In a world that often seems flat and one-dimensional Paul Elgie offers a tale that speaks to the depth of our reality. It is a story that transcends time and place and takes the reader on a memorable voyage that begins in the present and makes its way through medieval France to the ancient world. A well-researched story that carries the reader to several places – personal, historical and spiritual in order to speak of God's presence amidst the twists and turns of life as well as the life transforming power of God's grace and love captured in a pair of ancient and ordinary sandals.

—The Rev. Kevin Steeper
B.A., M.Div., S.T.B., M.Ed., M.A. Dipl. Spir. Dir.
Lakeshore United Church

Paul Elgie's experiences in drama, teaching and serving as a church elder, are woven together to create an interesting dialogue of fact & fiction. Readers will be drawn into the plot and emerge from the drama in a new way.

He captures the essence of life which challenges you spiritually to walk in 'His Sandals' as you love your neighbor as yourself. Like the woman from scripture, who touched the hem of the garment that flowed round him, the Sandals of Jesus, bring hope and change to those who come in contact with them.

The adventures of Eronte, remind you of the words of Muhammad Ali: 'The Service you do for others, is the rent you pay for your room here on Earth.'

—Rev. Jeffrey B. Hawkins B.A. M. Div.
Minister, Gorrie-Wroxeter United Church Pastoral Charge

W. PAUL ELGIE

HIS Sandals

HIS SANDALS

This is a work of fiction. Names, characters, places and incidents either are the product of the author's imagination or are used fictitiously, and any resemblance to actual persons, living or dead, businesses, companies, events, or locales is entirely coincidental.

Printed in Canada

ISBN: 978-1-4866-1369-4

Word Alive Press
131 Cordite Road, Winnipeg, MB R3W 1S1
www.wordalivepress.ca

Cataloguing in Publication may be obtained through Library and Archives Canada

With love to my darling wife Marilyn for her encouragement and loving, patient support when I was in the pangs of giving up, and also for her invaluable knowledge, generosity, and enthusiasm.

With thankful heart, I also dedicate this work to my daughters—Becky, Liz, Paula, and Krista—and my seven grandchildren—Micaela, Ben, Talia, Morgan, Victoria, Emma, and Sasha—for the joy they bring to my life.

Contents

Acknowledgements

With thanks to Larry Willard, for reading the first chapters of my book and encouraging me by pointing me in the right directions to further my publishing dreams. Also, thanks be to Ray Wiseman for his constructive advice.

ONE

The Beginning

"Treatorus, this man claims to be the Son of God. Nail him to the cross. Let him prove it!"

Grabbing a rusty iron spike and placing its sharply pointed end at the man's wrist, Treatorus yelled, "Hold him firmly! Press his arms tightly against the wooden cross! Watch him writhe and scream with pain!"

Treatorus, the most evil-minded of all legionnaires, brutally terrorized the convicted. He revelled in the pain he caused in crucifying people. The more he brutalized them, the more satisfaction he experienced.

His cruel eyes widened as he snarled, "Scream with anguish, you who claims to be King of the Jews. The louder the better."

The thick hammer slammed against the spike, forcing it through the man's wrist into the wooden cross. Treatorus violently forced the other three spikes. Yet this man did not cry out. He suffered in silence.

Stunned, Treatorus stumbled backwards in disbelief, as though pushed by a force unseen. This man on the cross was the only one ever not to scream in pain. Treatorus concentrated his attention, unable to believe the countenance on this man's face as he looked to heaven praying fervently to God His Father.

Could this man Jesus be the Messiah, the Son of God? Treatorus thought to himself. *He must be. I cruelly tortured him. He suffered excruciating pain. And even in his suffering, he prays to God.*

Treatorus stared directly into Jesus' eyes as the man prayed. "Father, forgive them, for they know not what they do."

During all these years, Treatorus had never experienced such contentment, joy, and happiness in his soul.

* * *

Flying on a Boeing 777 over the Atlantic Ocean to visit his daughter Lynne in northwestern France, Henry Marcelle pulled a piece of paper out of his inside jacket pocket. His daughter's email had told the story of an extremely old abbey built in the twelfth century in the rural French village of St. Sulpice de Foret.

> *Hi Dad. Learned a bit of history about this area. Check this out. There are old abbey ruins just outside of town. You might want to explore it. Love you dad. Can't wait to see you! :)*

He began to read the intriguing story about the abbey, translating it into English:

> Au debut du 12me siècle, un berger marchant dans la foret… *At the beginning of the twelfth century a shepherd walking through the forest came upon a statue of the Virgin Mary inside a blackbird's nest. He removed the statue and carried it carefully to his hovel. Seven times the Virgin Mary's statue returned by itself to the nest. To honour this happening, Our Ladies Chapel by the Water built in 1146 surrounded the tree containing the nest with the Statue of the Virgin Mary.*
>
> *A priest, Robert de Fustage, a disciple of Robert d'Abrissel, built a traditional Benedictine Celtic abbey beside the chapel. The first abbess, head of this nunnery, was Marie de Blois, a daughter of Stephen of England. Under the tutelage of the abbess, a monastery appeared on Monk's Hill. The nuns managed the spiritual side and the monks managed the temporal side. Construction of the abbey commenced during the reign of Cowan (1137–1171).*
>
> *Under the authority of Saint Siege and officially managed by Marie de Blois, the abbey's reputation spread throughout France and England. She became the chief justice in charge of the court, prison, and scaffold. The Abbey of Saint Sulpice ruled over the surrounding parishes. It became the owner of almost everything in the village,*

houses, dove cotes, cloister, woods, ponds, orchards, meadows, moors, pastures, and arable land. The money earned the abbey a fine reputation for helping people in need. This resulted in the abbey being given the privilege of obtaining from the famous Rennes forest their firewood, lumber, and wood to carve for the upkeep of their properties. Their cattle grazed in the forest.

Henry became more interested as he read further, having studied Stephen of Blois in a history course at the University of Western Ontario.

My first time in France, and at sixty-nine I'm actually going to see a twelfth-century abbey, he thought.

He remembered that King Stephen, a grandson of William the Conqueror, had become king when William Adelin had drowned in the *White Ship* sinking of 1120. The Abbess Marie de Blois could possibly have been Stephen's daughter, called Marie I, Countess de Boulogne. Could this Marie have been the abbess of the St. Sulpice abbey?

Brittany does have some history. There's nothing in Toronto of that vintage! He smiled to himself. *Except maybe me!*

His mood lightened, he read on.

The abbey began to decline when Brittany and France joined their territories. Catastrophe after catastrophe caused the abbey to be ruined. Fires in 1556, 1651, and 1701 caused great hardships. The great storm of 1616 destroyed the roof. The plague, the religious wars of 1595, and the famines, especially in 1661, brought about the abbey's end.

In later years, Marguerite d'Angennes governed the abbey for fifty-four years after the fire of 1651. With great effort she almost raised the abbey's influence back to its height. Her seventeenth-century portrait hangs on the wall of the Mayor's Council Chamber at St. Sulpice de Foret because of her rallying devotion to regaining the abbey's influence in the late 1600s.

Henry fell asleep despite the interesting commentary, transported in a dream to times and visions of years past.

"Henry, Henry! Welcome to our abbey, Henry. We've been waiting for you to help build the wall at the back of the altar. You're noted as a builder for placing the stones in a dry wall without mortar."

What was happening? The sky was darkening above the altar wall. Outside, he saw a cross on a hill.

I must get closer! *he thought.* My legs are weighing me down!

A man was suffering on that cross, his faithful followers crying out in horror as a soldier thrust spikes into his flesh.

He turned away, unable to watch. Soldiers were arguing over the man's sandals. He concentrated on placing stones quickly and efficiently. Soon the wall was finished.

As he turned to leave, he found himself drenched with sweat.

It was my Jesus! *he realized.*

The abbey crashed down in ruins.

"We are waiting, Henry," the voice said, "waiting for you at the abbey ruins."

A hand shook him vigorously. "Mr. Marcelle," the flight attendant said. "Mr. Marcelle, are you all right?"

TWO

The Amazing Discovery

Henry jolted awake, beads of sweat dripping from his forehead as the plane touched down at Charles de Gaulle airport. He shook off the reality of the dream.

Renting a car, he drove directly to his daughter's residence. When they met, they kissed each other on the cheek, hugged, held hands, and sat down on the couch in the living room. They talked into the wee morning hours.

"Honey, it's so nice to see you," he said. "I can't wait 'til morning light to visit the Chapel of Notre Dame du Nid au Merle. I feel like I already know the place. I studied King Stephen at Western and I want to see the place where I think his daughter officiated for many years."

"There's not much to look at, Dad," Lynne said. "The chapel is in ruins, with missing walls and grass floors, but I'm sure you'll enjoy it, with your passion for history."

"What have you learned about the area? Fill me in."

"Well, the landscapes and geography are impressive. Many cliffs and harbours indent the coast in Breton along the coastline," she said. "I read that the Romans came to Brittany from Great Britain in 51 B.C. It didn't join France until 1532."

Dad and daughter enjoyed a glass of French burgundy, caught up on news from home, and planned the next few days of sightseeing. Then Henry settled down for a good night's rest.

* * *

"Bonjour, Dad," Lynne said to him in the morning. "I have crepes with berries and crème."

"Mmm, delicious. Thanks, Lynne. I'm off to see the chapel ruins," Henry said. "I dreamed about it all night. My mind travelled all over the place, wondering what transpired during the abbey's existence. I can't wait to see the missing wall and the floor of grass, and maybe discover secrets of its history. I'm really intrigued."

"Enjoy this fresh country day, Dad! See you later."

Henry rushed out of the house, walking toward the remains of the chapel until he was out of breath. When he reached the village centre, he suddenly remembered the portrait of the abbess that supposedly hung in the village hall. He located the building and received permission to enter.

Indeed, a full-length portrait of Abbess Marguerite d'Angennes hung on the wall behind the mayor's upraised chair. The artist had filled the painting with expressive colour, depicting her in a very dignified manner. The image emanated her power, generosity, work ethic, and kindness. Her smile welcomed Henry, her bluish-green eyes looking straight at him and invading his soul. She appeared to be about five feet tall with a gentle physique obscured by her jet black habit, white around the neck, and headdress. Her right hand held her rosary as if she was fingering a bead in silent prayer. The other hand held a golden cross with the crucified body of Christ.

Above the classical painting, in clear block letters, was printed the Abbess' philosophy of leading her flock, in Jesus' own words:

> *"Love the Lord your God with all your heart and with all your soul and with all your mind." This is the first and greatest commandment. And the second is like it: "Love your neighbor as yourself." All the Law and the Prophets hang on these two commandments.*
>
> —Matthew 22:37–40

Digesting these two essential, life-enhancing commandments, Henry left the village centre, walking urgently, almost running, to reach the chapel.

Arriving at the ancient ruins, he squeezed through the half-rotted wooden door that had been frozen half-open for centuries. The ceiling of the nave was missing, along with the wall on the other side of the nave. Chipped rocks had crumbled at the base of the wall onto the uncut grass floor. A partially antiquated roof remained above the three altars in front of the bema, the main altar, with a smaller altar on each side. Through the lower half of the altars' outside wall, cattle grazed calmly in the field. The only complete walls were the ones around the wedged door.

Walking in knee-high grass along the back wall, Henry felt with bare fingers the rough boulders cut and placed without mortar, closely fitted with no space between. He admired, respected, and acknowledged the skilled artisans who had worked with only a chisel and hammer. He himself was a master stone mason, specializing in the building of dry stone walls.

Finally, after reverently rubbing his fingers along the rock in the wall, Henry respectfully knelt at the main altar, bowed his head, and started praying.

Henry thanked God through Jesus for the blessing of his life of sixty-nine years. He whispered a quiet prayer praising those who had lived in this convent and monastery through the centuries. He felt that every person who had entered these crumbling walls would marvel at the story the chapel secreted.

As he prayed, hands upraised toward heaven, a crack thundered, followed by a thump of something hitting the ground beside him. Saying "Amen," he opened his eyes to find at his feet an ancient, well-worn leather bag with a broad leather shoulder strap. Looking up, he discovered an open crevice in the wall from which the bag had fallen. Henry somehow knew he was expected to retrieve this relic.

"What is this?" he asked aloud. Where had it come from? Why had it dropped beside him?

Without hesitation, he bent down, picked up the bag, and carefully secured the strap over his shoulder. With no explanation, he felt his prayers answered. Christ's peace, contentment, and joy filled his whole being.

Standing reverently in front of the altar, he knelt again and prayed faithfully like never before, aware of God's all-powerful presence. Time seemed to be eternal.

Rising, he bowed once again, turned, and rushed out the half-open door. He headed quickly to inform his daughter what had taken place.

Breathlessly reaching her place, Henry climbed the steps to the side door by twos. "Lynne," he yelled, "come here!"

"You sound excited. What happened, Dad?"

Henry told the story in detail with both hands flying through the air, his voice and gestures revealing his excitement at the adventure at the ruined chapel.

"Look at this! It fell out of the wall and landed right beside me." He showed her the bag. "I have no idea what's inside. Holding it sure gave me a meaningful feeling."

Both reached to open the bag as if guided by a heavenly spirit. Opening the flap together, they lifted out a pair of ancient leather sandals. The insoles were darkened and marked with the pressure of sweat from feet trudging over many roads. The soles, rubbed smooth by sand pathways, were embedded with minute stones. The straps were frayed and cracks showed in the leather where its owner's feet had bent while stepping.

Lynne saw all this in a glance as she turned the sandals over in her hands. "Dad, these are ancient!"

Reaching in, she discovered thirty thin sheets of fine leather, fragile, yellowed with time, and engraved with extremely small French letters. Wrapped around the leather pages was a rolled-up paper tied securely with a green leather strap.

THREE

The Note Inscribed

"Dad, look what's in here!" Lynne exclaimed. "An old paper, yellowed and mouldy from age!"

Carefully unravelling the paper, they discovered a letter written in French. Lynne translated it.

Jesus Christ's sandals are in this bag. The story of how these sandals were given to Eronte, a homeless boy in Jerusalem, is well told.

"What!" Henry could hardly believe his ears. "The sandals of Christ! Could that be possible? Read it again, Lynne."

"That's what the letter says, Dad."

Jesus Christ's sandals are in this bag. The story of how these sandals were given to Eronte, a homeless boy in Jerusalem, is well told.

Sir Robert of Normandy, a French crusader, attacked the City of Jerusalem on June 6, 1099. While praying, thanking Almighty God for his army's success at St. Stephen's church, named after the first Christian martyr, the head priest presented Sir Robert a leather bag containing Jesus Christ's sandals and scrolls telling the story of Eronte. The priest asked Sir Robert and his knights to place this bag in care of a nunnery in France. Sir Hughes de Payne, returning from Jerusalem in 1161, gave this bag to me, asking that I and all the nuns guard this relic. The papyrus was cracking, falling apart, and disintegrating along the edges.

Fortunately, one of our nuns who had studied Hebrew translated the story into French. With our assistance, she transcribed the entire story on newly invented paper made from trees. Placing Jesus Christ's sandals in the original satchel, along with the story written in French and my explanatory letter to whoever is blessed with the sandals, I am placing the satchel in an opening in the upper part of the chapel's outside wall. The opening will be concealed by a stone.

All of us praise Almighty God and Lord Jesus for the peace, happiness, contentment, joy, and hope this gift has given us and to whomever discovers this Christian treasure.

Abbess Marie de Blois

"It seems the letter was written by the abbess in charge. Dad, do you believe she was King Stephen's daughter?"

"Yes. Well, at least I think so."

Mesmerized by the abbess' words, Henry and Lynne read aloud the story of Eronte.

FOUR

Eronte Alone

One afternoon while returning home, Eronte saw legionnaires standing in his family's courtyard. He quickly crouched down, shivering in fear, to hide behind the stone boulders of a nearby fence. Eronte's parents had warned him to beware of these soldiers.

What do they want? he wondered. *Where is my father? Is Mother inside? Why don't they send the soldiers away?*

After one more cursory glance around the courtyard and down the length of the dusty street, the soldiers marched off in the opposite direction from where Eronte was concealed.

Cowering in fear, he remained in his hiding place until dusk when he crept into the courtyard of his home and found it empty. His parents were gone. Nothing was left in the home to indicate anyone had ever lived there. Alone but resolute, Eronte kept watch until his little boy eyes, red-rimmed with tears, closed in frightened sleep. All that night and for the next few days, he hoped that a miracle would bring his parents back.

Determined to find his parents, Eronte searched the streets of Jerusalem every day. People he passed on the dirty back alleys wondered what had happened to this child, this young Jewish boy with dark and matted curly hair, clothes ragged and feet dusty. He was often sobbing. He fought other children in desperation for scraps of food, cunningly stealing to survive as he searched through the lower market street, alleyways, and bazaar stalls of the great city.

As the days lengthened to weeks, Eronte became hardened from the cruelty of others. Often he was the brunt of harsh language or beatings from shopkeepers.

"You! Boy! Get on with you! Get home where you belong!"

Even in the midst of this rough existence, Eronte remembered that his parents had taught him to respect the rights of others, and to treat others as he wished to be treated.

One day, while grabbing a fig from a vegetable stall, someone roughly grabbed his arm.

"Thief!" boomed the voice of Mr. Guandel, the shopkeeper. "You won't steal from my stall. Where are your parents?"

Eronte collapsed in fear with long held back tears. "I–I–I don't know, sir. One day I came home and the soldiers were there. My parents were gone. I can't find them."

"Hmph. Well, boy, I'll tell you what I'll do. You can deliver groceries to my customers, and as payment I'll feed you and let you sleep here under the cantaloupe table guarding my stalls."

Grabbing the hem of the man's robe, Eronte sputtered, "Thank you, sir, Mr. Guandel, I will work hard for you."

Even under these harsh circumstances, Eronte's thankful spirit and sense of duty helped him to survive. Outwardly he showed strength as he delivered fruit and vegetables, but inwardly he often felt sad.

One day, to Eronte's horror, as he passed Golgotha, he watched Roman legionnaires cruelly nail a man to the cross.

"Oh no!" Eronte yelled, recognizing the man. "No! Don't! Don't nail Jesus' hands... no!"

Falling on his knees in the dirt, tears streaming down Eronte's cheeks, he looked into the face of Christ.

Jesus is looking at me, he thought. *His eyes are smiling at me. How can He be, with all the cruelty done to Him? I love You, Jesus.*

"Jesus, I watched the Roman legionnaires march you to the synagogue," Eronte said. "You were tried and found guilty for claiming to be the Son of God. I thought Pilate would set You free. I cried as they forced You to carry the heavy wooden cross. Jesus, I love You."

The Roman legionnaires, oblivious to the crying child, began dividing Christ's clothes among themselves. One legionnaire took Jesus' outer robe, another Jesus' neck cloth, and the cruellest, a man named Legionnaire Treatorus, grabbed the sandals of Jesus Christ.

"These are mine!" Treatorus cried out.

The moment he grabbed Christ's sandals, Jesus, with a compassionate expression and forgiving eyes, prayed, "Father, forgive them, for they know not what they do."

Watching this teacher whom he had severely tortured pray for his forgiveness, Treatorus realized in his heart that he had to stop his treachery.

What should I do? Treatorus thought. *What has happened to my heart and mind? I must thank this Jesus for forgiving my cruelty. I have never felt contented and filled with joy and compassion before. Why must I treat others as I wish to be treated? And yet I must!*

Bowing low and falling to his knees, Treatorus wept. "I am so sorry. Thank You, Jesus. Your forgiveness, love, and compassion have made me a new person, reborn and renewed."

He then spotted a bedraggled boy standing stone-still, tears coursing down his face. Treatorus ran towards the boy, screaming with urgency.

Seeing the cruel legionnaire running towards him, Eronte shook with fear.

"Boy, halt!" Treatorus called. "Stop now! Come here!"

"Y–y–yes, sir."

"Son, forgive me for frightening you. I am the man who crucified Jesus. And then He forgave me! Seeing you, in rag clothing, I had to do something good. Take these sandals of Jesus. The sandal man three blocks over will buy them. Tell him I sent you. You will get a good price. You can buy some food and clothes."

Treatorus, feeling for the first time that he had accomplished some good, had happy tears running down his face.

Bowing low, Eronte whispered, "Thank you, sir."

Looking directly at Christ, crucified and nailed to the cross, Eronte thought to himself, *This man did not deserve to be crucified.*

The boy bowed his head. "Thank You for Your sandals, Jesus. I will make the best use of them that I can."

Eronte disappeared down the dusty street.

A nearby centurion, seeing what had happened, stared at Jesus, praised God, and proclaimed, "This was a righteous man. Surely He was the Son of God!"

Jesus called out in a loud voice, "Father, into Your hands I commit My spirit." Once He had said this, He breathed His last.

FIVE

Emontial

Emontial, a tight-fisted, greedy, cold-hearted man in his late fifties, despised all things that brought happiness. His cold grey eyes and bulbous, purple-veined nose combined to form a less than desirable face.

He would secretly pick people to work for him whom he wanted to enslave. He loaned them money on the pretence of being their benefactor, telling them they needn't pay for a year, and then without warning called the money in. When they weren't able to pay, he followed the Roman law and enslaved them.

Every day Emontial walked purposefully around Jerusalem, revelling in the misery he caused. He thoroughly enjoyed watching his slaves being beaten for not working hard enough to suit him. His workers were paid minimal wages and expected to work to their maximum. The more downtrodden the workers and his slaves were, the more gratification Emontial felt.

Emontial was the richest man in Jerusalem, and also the most hated. He owned many businesses, a chariot factory, a construction company, shops in the upper city which sold luxury imported foods, and many other high-profit entities. Unfortunately, he didn't appreciate the money or influence he had. He hated everyone, and therefore he had no friends. The only seemingly friendly characters were those who could take advantage of his prideful state of mind and enhance themselves with his wealth.

On this day, he decided to walk through the back alley of his slum. It contained old stone buildings with doors askew. Crumbling walls plastered with watered limestone tumbled into courtyards. Window shutters hung torn and tattered. Steps to the roofs were uneven and crumbling. Many roofs had broken beams. Smells of human remains and decay filled the air.

Here Emontial charged the highest rent possible for places he never improved. If anyone complained about the filthy condition of their abode, he kicked them out immediately, without any return on their rent, or raised their rent.

"You over there, don't complain," he called to someone in a grating voice. "Your walls are crumbling! Fix them! Don't expect me to. If you want to live in my fine houses, pay your rent. Your rent is overdue. Do you expect me to pay it?"

"Please, sir. May I have just two more days?"

"No! By sundown tonight, or I'll send my men to force you out."

"But sir, I won't have the money for two more days. Please, I have a wife and two children."

"Who cares! By sundown tonight!"

With a sinister smile, Emontial continued his slow walk, pleased with himself. His slum looked increasingly poverty-stricken.

Suddenly, four men rushed out of the shadows behind him. "You scum! You deserve to be killed!"

"What! Who do think you are? Get out of my way! I'll have all four of you thrown out! Move, now!"

The men menacingly drew their circle closer and knocked Emontial to the ground.

"How dare you knock me down?" As Emontial struggled to get up, they hit and kicked him with such force that he doubled over in pain. "No! Stop, I demand it!"

With knuckles bared, each one punched Emontial more vehemently, forcing him to the ground.

"You'll never hurt anyone again," one man shouted. "You monster! You cruel, inhuman beast, we will be justified if we have killed you. Hit him harder!"

As he lay motionless on the ground, all four spit in Emontial's bloodied face. Thinking he was dead, they robbed him of his purse, outer garments, and turban.

"Run, before the legionnaires come," said the ringleader.

They rushed away, feeling they had rid the poor people of this cruel and dishonest landowner who had made their lives a pity to behold.

Thus Emontial found himself bloodied, beaten, and robbed by the very men who lived in his rundown hovels.

* * *

Eronte, his mind still filled with the horrific scene of Jesus on the cross, thought about the forgiveness and saving of Legionnaire Treatorus, and the gift of Christ's sandals. He knew he still had to deliver groceries quickly, or be beaten and starved by Mr. Guandel for his tardiness.

I'm really in trouble now, he thought, trying to figure out the quickest way back to the market. *Mr. Guandel is going to be so mad!*

Eronte decided to take a shortcut through the back alley of a poverty-stricken area. As he turned a corner into this dilapidated community, he saw four ruffians beating a richly dressed man almost to the point of death, and then racing away.

Creeping out from behind his hiding place, Eronte wondered what to do. Should he find a legionnaire? There weren't any around.

Maybe I can help, he thought.

Eronte crouched down beside the man, who seemed lifeless. He placed Jesus' sandals on the man's chest and his neck cloth over the man's swollen face, beaten to a pulp.

The cloth moved slowly.

Eronte tore the cloth off the man's battered face.

Emontial opened his eyes and weakly uttered, "Please, help me."

Six

Peaceful Wellness

Emontial started to breathe normally. His eyes focused and his whole demeanour changed, replacing his terrible snarling continence with quiet peace. With a grateful heart, he stared wide-eyed at the boy.

"Thank you," Emontial said. "Please, help me home."

"Where do you live, sir?"

"We return to the main street at the end of this alley. Turn right. And keep walking."

Wincing in pain, Emontial lifted himself painstakingly to his feet. With Eronte supporting him, they limped ever so slowly over the dusty cobblestones toward the luxury mansions of the upper city.

"Two more streets, then turn left. But stop a minute. Let me rest on that stone wall."

A few minutes passed as he rested, deep in thought, Emontial reflected on his life. Because of the beating, he now realized how precious life was. *Why am I still alive? Maybe I have been doing wrong. What has happened? I sense a new peace within me. That sounds impossible, but it's true.*

He turned his attention to the boy. "How have you, a small lad, made me feel this way in spite of my injuries?"

Panicking, Eronte urged him to continue on. "Sir, please, get up, I must hurry or I'll be in trouble."

With renewed effort, Emontial stumbled forth. At the next corner, they turned left and stopped in front of an impressive house with a substantial stone fence, solid gate, and wide courtyard with a stone walkway and colourful garden flowers.

When they entered through the gate, the boy said, "I must get back to Mr. Guandel's vegetable market. I still have a great many orders to deliver. If I don't finish my work, he will beat me and not feed me."

"Wait, boy! Wait! Where do you live?"

Without answering, the boy ran at a leopard's pace, disappearing into the distance.

SEVEN

Cantaloupes

Eronte rounded the corner to the vegetable market as fast as his little legs could carry him, fearing he would be punished for being so long and not finishing his deliveries.

Mr. Guandel waited at the market door. He immediately grabbed Eronte and picked him up. "Where have you been?" he yelled in a cruel voice. "My customers are waiting for you. I shall lose money because of your tardiness."

"I'm sorry, I'm sorry. I helped a man who was hurt."

"I don't care what you did." He slapped Eronte harshly across the face. "Get those deliveries done! Then I'll think about feeding you and letting you sleep under the cantaloupe table. Run!"

Eronte placed Jesus' sandals under the cantaloupe table, picked up two grocery piles, and dashed out the door.

Guandel reached under the table to see what the boy had so carefully placed there.

"Where did the boy get these sandals?" he asked himself. "What has he been up to? Wait 'til he gets back here."

A short time later, the boy rushed back to the shop and grabbed some more parcels. Just as he was about to run out the door again, Guandel yelled, "Stop! Come here, Eronte! I want to talk to you."

The boy stopped, shivering, and backed away, fearing that Guandel would strike him again.

"Eronte, I picked up your sandals. Where did you get these? Did you steal them?"

"They were Jesus' sandals," Eronte said. "Jesus, the man on the cross. He said, 'Forgive them for they know not what they do.' Treatorus, the meanest legionnaire, heard Jesus say that. Then Treatorus looked at me, gave me the sandals, and told me to sell them to the sandal maker. But these are Jesus' sandals. They're special to me, so I kept them. I loved Jesus."

Guandel, astonished at the way Treatorus had changed after experiencing Jesus' forgiveness, thought to himself, *There must have been something special about this teacher, Jesus.* He picked up the sandals. *Maybe I shouldn't have treated this boy so cruelly. He works hard for me, and I couldn't do without him.*

"Eronte, deliver as many parcels as you can," he said at last. "When you come back, I'll feed you."

Stunned at the change in Guandel, all Eronte could utter was, "Thank you. Thank you, thank you, sir!"

Eronte worked hard into the evening to finish all the deliveries. During his travels, he asked himself many questions. What had happened to Guandel? Why had he been kind? Could it have been Jesus' sandals?

Those sandals of Jesus help people, Eronte concluded. *They brought Emontial back from the dead. What should I do with them? I won't sell them to the sandal maker.*

With a full stomach, Eronte curled up to sleep under the cantaloupe table, exhausted from the eventful day.

EIGHT

Changes and Chariots

The next morning, Eronte awoke to a well-dressed servant towering above him. "I spoke with Guandel and he gave you leave for one day."

"Who are you?"

"My name is Genitos, charioteer for Emontial. For saving his life, Emontial instructed me to bring you back to his house to thank you in person. He requests you to bring the sandals."

Going outside with Genitos, Eronte beheld the most lavish chariot, trimmed with ivory and gold leaf. The charioteer directed him to climb in, then galloped the horses all the way to Emontial's home.

"Wow!" Eronte said. "Wow, the horses go fast! Can they go any faster?"

Chuckling to himself, Genitos urged the horses on with a flick of the reins. "Go faster, boys, for this young man."

Standing by the gate, Emontial welcomed them with a warm, inviting smile. He rushed to help Eronte climb off the chariot. "Thank you for saving my life. I see that you brought the sandals. Please, can I carry them?"

Eronte hesitantly handed the sandals to Emontial, explaining that they had belonged to Jesus, the healer who the soldiers had nailed to a cross.

"A legionnaire gave them to me," Eronte said.

Emontial held the sandals. *They somehow emanate with love and forgiveness, helping me to feel like the man I want to be*, he thought. *Could they have brought me back to life?*

Joining his large, manicured hand with Eronte's small, rough one, Emontial led the boy into a white-floored courtyard surrounded by a high decorated wall. He motioned the boy to sit in the portico.

"Young man, I thank you from deep in my heart for saving my life. I have never felt as good about being alive as I do now. I used to be proud of being the most miserly person. I prided myself on my cruelty, punishing, provoking, and torturing others. From now on, I'll try to be kind and thoughtful. My new purpose in life is to help others less fortunate. I thank you for placing Jesus' sandals on my chest when I was dying." Emontial lowered himself, planting his knee on the white stones, and looked directly into Eronte's eyes. He held the boy's hand tightly. "Young man, please help me fully become the kind, loving, caring, and generous person I wish to be."

"Sure, I'll help you. If I can!"

Emontial rose. Still gently holding the boy's hand, he led Eronte into the centre room of the spacious house.

Eronte was confused. Why was this man smiling, with tears running torrentially down his cheeks?

Emontial sobbed for ten minutes before speaking. He cupped the boy's hand with both of his hands. "Eronte, please work for me. Without your help, people will believe that whatever I do is for my benefit, not theirs. They wouldn't believe me, but they'll believe you. And I wouldn't blame them. I've hurt so many people in the past, and laughed as I made them suffer."

"B–but I work for Mr. Guandel."

"Yes, I know. I will talk to Guandel and see if we can figure that out. I wish to be a generous man, and I need your help to gain people's respect. You are young, just a boy, but I feel confident that with the sandals of Jesus, you can change me."

"Me, sir?"

"Yes. I know you exist in a very harsh environment and have learned how to survive. Come, live with me. Help me forgive myself. Give me the courage to ask forgiveness from all the people I have harmed over the years. Together, you and I, with the power of Jesus through His sandals, can create miracles for others."

Surprised, Eronte hesitated. Then he gave the man a tight hug. "Sir, thank you for being so kind! Can I have another ride in your huge chariot?"

"Absolutely," Emontial responded with a chuckle. "We'll ride to visit my factories. But first we'll go to Guandel to explain our plan."

With one large hand clutching a small one, they rushed out the door where Genitos stood at attention, guarding the ornately decorated chariot.

Arriving at the vegetable market, still clutching Eronte's hand, Emontial ushered the boy inside the market.

"Guandel, my name is Emontial."

"I know who you are," the shopkeeper said. "The cruellest enemy of many of my customers! You would have them starve. Eronte, let go of that evil man's hand. Come to me. I will protect you."

Eronte started to speak, but Emontial butted right in. "Guandel! Listen!"

"Get out of here right now, you wretch, or I'll have the Roman legionnaires remove you forcefully."

"You are absolutely right in chastising me, Guandel. I was all that and more," Emontial said. "Yesterday, while walking through my slums, several tenants brutally attacked me and left me for dead. At the point of death, Eronte helped me to stand and saved my life. He placed Jesus Christ's sandals on my chest. Somehow I felt the power of love and healing go through me. In order to thank Eronte, I sent Genitos to bring him to my house. Now I return with him to ask that you allow him to live with me. I need his help, because people like you would never believe that I could change. My new purpose is to do good, not evil. Please, allow me to raise this boy, to thank him for saving my life."

Guandel gave this some consideration. "I would like to help you, but I have two questions. Can you be trusted to look after this boy? And who will deliver my vegetables? I rely on my boy to help me. He works hard and is really good with the customers."

"I can solve that easily. Trust me! I promise you, I will treat the boy as a son. I will have one of my trusted workers, not a slave, be trained by Eronte over a period of time, and I will pay that worker for one year to deliver your vegetables. Will that be satisfactory?"

Guandel extended his hand towards Emontial. "Yes! Follow me to my home behind the market. We will seal our agreement over a glass of wine."

* * *

After the visit, Genitos drove Eronte to the chariot factory.

"What do you need this big building for?" Eronte asked. "Is it yours?"

Genitos chuckled. "This is a chariot factory. We manufacture the best, fastest, and most reliable chariots in the Roman Empire. Come in and I'll show you."

Throughout the tour, Genitos explained in detail how each piece was assembled.

The boy's face lit up with inquisitiveness over every aspect of the factory. "What does that do? What's the round thing for? Why are big knives attached to the wheels?"

"Eronte, yesterday Senator Quintus of Rome ordered one thousand chariots, the greatest number ever ordered at one time," Genitos said. "He is responsible for purchasing all Roman weapons of war."

Eronte beamed as they left the factory and climbed into the chariot.

"Can I drive the chariot?" Eronte asked.

Genitos grinned and handed the boy the horses' reins. He watched carefully as Eronte drove, impressed at how quickly the boy learned.

When they arrived home, Emontial showed the boy into a separate room with a bed of his own. "This is your room, Eronte."

"A real bed? For me? I've never slept in a bed like this!"

Overwhelmed, Eronte flung arms tightly around Emontial's waist. All he could remember was sleeping on the floor under the cantaloupe table.

Eronte curled up in luxurious exhaustion and fell asleep immediately.

Watching the sleeping child, Emontial tearfully recalled the events of recent days. He was aware of a new, positive way of life, and knew he was on the brink of accomplishing it.

The sandals of Jesus seem to have power, he thought. *I know they can't be magical, but there is something. I'm going to find out about this Jesus and learn where His power comes from, and how His message of love and forgiveness changes lives.*

NINE

School Beginnings

One morning several months later, Emontial woke Eronte and explained over breakfast that in order to help like he had promised, Eronte must attend school for several years. Emontial had chosen a famous school in Rome that educated bright students, because the boy showed a spark of brilliance by the way he quickly understood new ideas.

Emontial summoned Genitos, with Eronte by his side. "Genitos, I commission you for the next four years to be the boy's guide, protector, adviser, and friend. Take him to Rome. All has been prepared for you there."

"I will do as you wish, Emontial. Do I have leave to make my preparations for the journey?"

"Yes, and Godspeed, Genitos. Eronte will be ready within the hour. I know you will provide my boy with wise counsel."

Bowing deeply, Genitos left Emontial and his adopted son.

Turning his attention to Eronte, Emontial spoke in crisp, definite words. "Eronte, I had a tanner construct a special leather bag with a wide neck strap made of the finest, strongest material. Keep this bag with you at all times. Protect it, because it contains Jesus' sandals. You and I both know that the sandals of Jesus remind us to help people follow God's commandment: treat your neighbour as you would like to be treated."

"Yes, sir. We know the great power in Jesus' sandals, but I would be afraid to lose them while I'm at school. Please, guard the sandals for me while I'm in Rome."

"If you wish, that would be an honour for me. Come with me while I safely stow the sandals inside the chest in my special room. And now, young man, Genitos awaits. Off with you."

With a quick hug, and a wave over his shoulder, Eronte walked out the door to a new adventure. Emontial stood on the porch steps, wiping moisture from his eyes as he waved goodbye.

Genitos drove the chariot to the harbour at Asquelon to board the galley, which was owned by Emontial. It sailed out of the harbour, bound for Rome.

The blue, cloud-free sky continued for the first three days. On the fourth day, a thunderstorm of epic proportions struck. Waves twenty to forty feet high threw the ship wildly from valley to mountaintop. Sailors wrestled with lowering the sails, and Captain Ingo and his first mate struggled to right the ship with four strong hands clutching the wheel.

The boat was about to break apart due to the fierceness of the terrible storm. Everyone feared for their lives.

Captain Ingo ordered everyone on deck. Thrust into the captain's arms, Eronte pressed against him as hard as he could. A vision of Jesus surfaced in his mind. He remembered staring into Jesus' face when he had received the sandals and knew that His spirit would help him now.

Eronte prayed in a loud voice: "Jesus, please save us all from this storm."

The winds abated, the waves lessened, and the storm ceased within minutes. Calm weather returned. A warm wind filled the sails to capacity, pushing the galley at full speed to Rome.

Eronte, Genitos, Captain Ingo, and all aboard were witnesses to the miracle. In awe, they fell to their knees with a silent prayer of thanks to God for sparing their lives.

TEN

Seeking a New Life in Jesus

Emontial, while sitting alone eating breakfast on his porch, realized that in spite of all his worldly holdings, his mind was not content, and his life seemed empty. He missed his only friends, who were on their way to Rome. What could he do to learn how to be a happy, resourceful person?

Time passed slowly until out of the blue came an exciting thought: *I will search for someone who knew Jesus, the healer who was crucified, and whose sandals Eronte placed in my safekeeping.*

Emontial, quivering with excitement, left his house and walked at a fast pace to the business centre of Jerusalem. Arriving there, he questioned himself on how to approach his quest. There might be real danger if he asked where he could find a friend of Jesus, because Jesus had been crucified. Would the Sanhedrin or their spies have him arrested, charged, and jailed? Was there anyone he had met in business over the years whom he could trust?

Many names passed through his mind, but one rested there. At least many years ago, he and Nicodemus had made many mutually rewarding deals together. Would Nicodemus still be in business?

He found Nicodemus' shop still there, and it was open. Entering the doorway, Emontial saw the man he'd come for. When Nicodemus had finished doing business with a customer, Emontial walked up to him and held out his hand.

"Nicodemus, friend," he greeted warmly, "what a pleasure to see you again after all these years."

"Emontial! I haven't seen you or heard anything about you for twenty years. You haven't changed a bit. What brings you here to see me? Knowing you so well, you must have an important reason."

"Yes, I do. But our business must be kept in the strictest confidence. Would you agree to that? No one else must know what we discuss."

"Emontial, my curiosity is aroused. You have my word." Nicodemus grabbed Emontial's hand and shook it strongly.

Emontial grabbed both of his friend's hands. "Who is Jesus, the man crucified by the Roman legionnaires? Can you find me someone who knew Him? I want to learn all I can about Him."

"You're right. It can be dangerous to ask questions about Jesus." Nicodemus freed his hands from Emontial's tight grip. "Come back here in a week. I'll look into things. Don't mention our conversation to anyone."

Emontial agreed and left the shop, walking hurriedly home.

Sitting on his porch with a glass of wine, he wished the week would pass quickly. Many questions filled his thoughts.

Did the attackers kill me? Did I die? Did the boy bring me back to life through the power of Jesus' sandals? Why have I changed, wanting to be a loving man instead of a hating man? Was it because I realize the great privilege of being alive? Why do I feel happier being kind to people than being cruel and seeing others suffer? What will I learn about the healer Jesus?

The week passed slowly.

On their designated meeting day, Emontial arrived early to meet Nicodemus. Nicodemus appeared late and remained icily quiet. The silence bothered Emontial.

"What is wrong, Nicodemus? You haven't said a word to me."

"You charlatan," Nicodemus said. "You dared to come here to ask about Jesus, the Master who treated people kindly, teaching them, healing them, and serving those who needed help. I have found out that you have changed from the kind of man I knew. You have become a killer, a murderer, a thief of thieves, a selfish liar and cheat, a slave beater, a torturer. I'm ashamed to even admit I know you. You are not the man I knew so well. Don't say a word to me. Get out of here. I don't want to be in your presence ever again."

"Wait, Nicodemus, listen. You're right, I was that man, even worse than you describe, but a boy carrying the sandals of Jesus saved my life. My life changed completely, and now I've become a man who wishes to treat everyone as I would like to be treated."

"Everyone I talked to hates you for your cruel behaviour. You lie! I don't believe you have changed. Get out of my shop immediately and never return, or I'll call a legionnaire and have you put in prison."

On bended knee, with tears flowing, Emontial begged that he be allowed the opportunity to prove that his life had changed, that he now helped one and all to live better lives.

"Prove it," Nicodemus challenged. "I'll give you one chance, but one chance only. Show me that your life has changed."

"I'll take you to my former slums and let you talk to my tenants. I'll take you to my factories and let you ask questions of everyone, including my slaves. I'll take you to my house and let you speak to my servants. That's just a start."

"Let's do it right now, before you have the opportunity to frighten your workers into submission. I don't believe a word you say. The people I questioned pegged you as the cruellest man who ever lived in Jerusalem."

"Follow me to my chariot, and you'll see that I do not lie."

They left the shop and travelled quickly to the restored slums.

"Where are the slums?" Nicodemus asked when they arrived. "You're trying to trick me! These places are better than most homes."

"These were the worst slums in Jerusalem. I hired the tenants to repair the broken down buildings. I paid each tenant a fair wage and provided funds for materials. Their rent was reduced, and in fact many received rent back that I had overcharged them. I've insisted they treat each other as they would like to be treated. Look for yourself at the results!"

Nicodemus was surprised, but still suspicious. He could hardly believe what he was seeing. He wasn't totally convinced. "Take me to one of your factories."

"The sewing factory is close by. We'll go there first."

Their chariot stopped in front of a long building where pleasant music could be heard. Entering the doorway, they saw several hundred women working diligently, young and old, each humming or singing quietly.

Nicodemus picked out a woman and questioned her. "Do you like working here?"

She stopped humming, eyes shining, and answered cheerily. "I do. Emontial pays us well. We sew at our own pace and are proud of the garments we make." She smiled at Emontial. "Hi, Emontial. It's nice to have you drop by. We wish you would come more often."

Nicodemus was speechless as they slowly left.

"I'll take you to my prize chariot factory," Emontial said. "Rome awarded me the job of building the largest, most effective and deadly war chariots for the Roman legionnaires."

It took some time to travel to the plant outside Jerusalem. Emontial toured Nicodemus through the large factory where over one thousand people were employed. Conversations and laughter could be heard from every corner of the building.

Exiting, Nicodemus exclaimed, "Take me back to my office. I've seen enough. I thank you for showing me the truth about your new life, and for not lying about your past. You have changed. Whatever—or whoever—changed you is very powerful."

Emontial's chariot drove through the streets to the shops of the upper city, returning Nicodemus to his place of business.

"Goodbye for now, Emontial. I will pursue your inquiry and send someone to your home in the next few days."

* * *

A week later, a well-dressed man appeared at Emontial's home to take him to meet Nicodemus at an inn in a nearby town.

"Welcome, Emontial," Nicodemus said once they were alone. "Follow me. I will introduce you to a disciple of Jesus."

They travelled together to a private home in the middle of a grove of fig trees and were heartily greeted by the owner.

"Emontial, this is Joseph of Arimathea."

"Welcome, Emontial," Joseph said. "Nicodemus asked me to tell you about Jesus. Why do you want to know about our Messiah?"

"Joseph, I'm here because a homeless lad, who had just witnessed Jesus forgive those who cruelly crucified Him, found me left for dead on the ground. He placed on my chest the sandals of Jesus, given to him by the legionnaire Treatorus. He then placed his neckerchief over my face. When it moved, the boy realized that I was alive. He assisted me to my feet and accompanied me home. When I knew that I lived again, a new appreciation of life overcame me. I knew that my life had to change in the way I treated people."

Joseph smiled at his story. "Emontial, Jesus was God's Son. God gave us His Son to teach us how to atone for all our sins, and live joyfully."

"I am thankful to have met you, Joseph, and more than ever thankful to be alive," Emontial said. "Will you please teach me more about Jesus? I want to learn everything about His teachings and how I can lead the best life I can, and to forgive myself of the terrible cruelties I imposed on people in the past."

"Jesus taught us God's two greatest commandments. First, to love God with all your heart, soul, and mind, and second, to treat your neighbour as you would like to be treated. Nicodemus tells me you have repented and are showing your love for God by treating your neighbours kindly, helping people to live better lives."

Nicodemus nodded. "Yes, that's right. After all the terrible things I heard about Emontial, he has proved to be a changed man."

"Thank you for your trust in me, Nicodemus," Emontial said. "Joseph, I want to learn all about your Messiah."

"Emontial, meet us here in a week at the same time. Nicodemus, myself, and others will pray for you. You have come a long way. Jesus has blessed you."

Emontial returned home with a thankful heart.

ELEVEN

At Romulus

Theopolus, proctor of the famous Romulus school of higher learning, waited expectantly for the ship to dock. He wanted to find out about his newest foreign student, whose benefactor was to pay double the fees charged for a regular student.

Eronte would spend the next four years at Romulus, until he was a young man of eighteen. Learning to read and write in Roman and Greek would be his first challenge. He would be taught how to fight, survive in combat, and outthink an opponent. One essential skill was to be humble but proud of yourself, to the extent that you always strove to overcome any endeavour.

As Eronte and Genitos disembarked, Theopolus introduced himself. "Welcome, Eronte. We look forward to developing your character and preparing you for the challenges of life." He turned his eyes to the boy's keeper. "Have we met before? You look vaguely familiar. Many years ago, a Grecian lad by the name of Genitos attended a similar school in Greece. In a championship match with Romulus, he could have scored the final goal but passed the ball to a fellow player instead. I remember this boy because of his sportsmanship and giving attitude. He was always the first to embrace players of the opposing team and assist when injuries occurred."

"Yes, that was me," Genitos said humbly. "Many years ago. We can talk about that later. I'm here as Eronte's protector, and I need to get him settled."

Theopolus furrowed his brow at Genitos, deciding to let the matter rest for the moment.

Arriving at Romulus, where only boys of the upper class studied, such as the sons of senators, Eronte's eyes widened. His body shook with trepidation as he sensed the coldness within these walls.

Ushered into Theopolus' office, he felt the stony atmosphere. He stood stiffly before the proctor's imposing desk.

"How old are you?" the proctor probed.

"Sir, I turned fourteen seven days ago."

"What is your educational background?"

"My mother and father taught me to read, write, and do sums until I was eight. Then they disappeared. I never saw them again."

"Very tragic! What did you do?"

"I searched for them. I lived in the streets, fought other boys for food, and slept wherever I found a place. One day I was caught stealing figs. The owner had me deliver groceries. He fed me and allowed me to sleep under the cantaloupe table in his shop. I was also the night guard."

"Explain why you are here."

"Emontial is the gentleman who has sent me here. When I saw several men beating him, I helped him. Then he took me to live with him. He calls me his adopted son."

"Very interesting. But enough! First we need to find your place in the class."

"My place, sir?"

The proctor had Eronte read, write, and solve some mathematical questions. To his surprise, he was impressed by the boy's sensible, down to earth answers. Theopolus knew Eronte was far more mature than other boys his age.

The proctor stood and reached out his hand. "Welcome to Romulus. I will personally show you the school, your classroom, the sports grounds, and your lodging. There are forty boys in the school—ten, including you, in your class." The proctor dismissed Genitos with a wave of his hand. "Genitos, go. We will contact you if necessary."

Rushing over, Eronte clutched his friend around the waist. "Genitos, I wish you wouldn't leave. I will really miss you." He straightened up. "I will be strong like you taught me."

Genitos, knowing the place of a slave, kept silent and smiled warmly at Eronte. He then turned and left immediately.

"Eronte, at Emontial's request, you will spend four years learning all you can about economics, defensive fighting, and civic life pertaining to

Roman and Greek politics and culture," Theopolus said. "The other boys arrive tomorrow. Come with me, and I will show you around the school. First we will visit the sports field."

Eronte wiped away a tear, squared his shoulders, and followed after Theopolus. "Thank you, sir. I saw a circular gravel track about two thousand paces round with a field in the centre. Is that the sports field?"

"Yes. Our sports program consists of practicing different sports every afternoon. We design each sport in a way to strengthen one's mind, body, and soul. By the time you leave here, you will be extremely fit. Your physical program will be customized to your personal strengths. You will run, jump, leap, box, and wrestle. You will defend yourself with your hands, legs, and especially your head. You will throw the discus and the spear. You will learn to fight effectively with a sword and shield. You will learn how to ride a horse and drive a war chariot. In four years, you will be prepared to succeed in this challenging world we live in. Do you have any questions?"

"When do I start?"

"Your first day is tomorrow, when the other boys arrive. Next I will take you to your classroom."

Arriving at the classroom, Eronte stared into a porch with uncomfortable-looking stone seats. The bleakness of the cold walls and the starkness of the porch chilled Eronte to the bone.

"A Greek educator, my slave, will teach you reading, writing, and mathematics," Theopolus said. "You will have an abacus to learn mathematics, and for writing you will have a stylus and wax tablet. As you advance, you will be taught political theory, even going to the senate to see and hear the senators conducting their governmental duties. You will finally study the writings of Cicero and other great philosophers. You will attend school every day from daybreak until sundown, except for holidays. You will be allowed to go home for a few days in the summer.

"One final thing you must start doing immediately is be on time, or early, to all the events you must attend. Do exactly as you are told and learn quickly what you are being taught. My educator will beat you harshly for any small offence. If you get something wrong, you will be caned. If you continue to misbehave by not learning, you will be held down and beaten with a leather whip."

Shivering, Eronte stared silently at the proctor, holding back tears.

"Follow me, Eronte. Let us now go see where you will sleep."

Arriving at his sleeping quarters, Eronte saw ten single beds. He found the one with his name on it in the far corner with a small stone table. The bed was barely big enough for him to lie in, with a thin straw mattress and small pillow.

"You now have time to walk around the school," Theopolus said. "I will see you at supper. Be on time. Enjoy the rest of the day. School starts at sunrise tomorrow."

Eronte didn't know what to think or do as the proctor left the room. As he flopped down on his bed, thoughts swirled in his mind. *What will happen to me? When will I get to go home? I miss Genitos and Emontial. I'm lonely. It sounds like a very hard school, but I will do my best to succeed as I promised.*

Getting up, he decided to walk around the school and check everything out.

* * *

At dawn the next morning, Eronte arrived at the classroom porch. Here he found a Greek slave teacher and nine classmates already seated. His fellow students all had parents from the wealthiest political and business class. The other nine boys, obviously friends from childhood, stared at him in a snobbish way. They whispered to each other as though to say "Why has this strange-looking kid with a big nose and different clothing been allowed to attend our elite school?"

Only the educator slave spoke aloud, instructing him to sit at the back. Alone.

During the lesson, Eronte understood nothing of the political theory being taught. Upon completion of the class, the teacher instructed Eronte to stand up and tell the class what he had learned. Eronte stood, shaking in fear because he didn't understand. He couldn't explain in detail what had been taught. To his fearful surprise, the educator grabbed him, made him pull his clothes down to expose his bare backside, and bent him over. A thin wooden cane struck him twelve times, causing severe pain and bleeding. Then he was told to sit down and pay attention.

Humiliated and hurting, Eronte sat down, holding back tears. The other boys laughed. They had been taught the same political lesson by their parents.

In the afternoon, the proctor marched the boys to the sports field. He instructed the boys to run the track as fast as they could, throw the javelin and discus to the best of their ability, fight in hand-to-hand combat, box, and wrestle. Eronte ran and fought adequately due to his homeless years, but the boys made shaming gestures when he failed to throw the javelin and discus properly. All Eronte could do was suffer the shame of inadequacy as his classmates scorned him. Although Eronte tried to be friendly, the other boys isolated him.

On the first political holiday, Genitos visited and took Eronte out to the country.

Tears flowed down Eronte's face. "Genitos, I hate school! The educator beats me! The boys laugh at me! Please, take me home to Emontial."

Genitos gently but firmly shook his head. "I swore an oath to Emontial that I would make a man of you. Therefore, it is not possible for you to go home, but I will train you to be an athlete."

And so Eronte began intensive training in all aspects of every sport. Every holiday, and there were several during the year, Genitos trained Eronte in the finer points of physical education. The boy was amazed to discover that Genitos was truly a well-trained athlete. Eronte trained hard, and by the end of the first year he had come to be in the middle of his class. Once school began for the third year, the proctor and Eronte's classmates realized that Eronte had gained much strength and skill that summer. He was as practiced and skilled as the lead boy.

The lead boy, who had always been the leader, didn't like his position challenged. In hand-to-hand combat, he started a fight with Eronte as if in real mortal combat.

Eronte knew he could beat the boy, but thinking maturely, he decided, *I will get to the point where he knows I can beat him, and then I will miss. I'll let him knock me down and he will win. He will save face and no other pupil will dare to attack either him or me.*

Eronte swung his powerful fist, missing his target on purpose by an inch. The other boy took advantage and knocked Eronte down, thus winning the fight. The victor reached down, grabbed Eronte's hand for the first time, and pulled him upright.

"You are a real man," the boy said. "You fought a good fight! Let me shake your hand!" Then, with his arm around Eronte's shoulder, he whispered in a conspiratorial voice, "I know you let me win."

The other pupils were shocked at their leader's action. They all shook Eronte's hand in turn, and congratulated him on his hard work and achievement.

At the end of his third year, Eronte was tied at the top of the class in every subject, including sports and academics. Finally, upon completion of his fourth year, the proctor, teacher, and classmates all voted Eronte top boy in their class.

The day before school ended, Theopolus met with Eronte and Genitos formally in his office.

"Eronte, I'm very proud that my Greek slave, along with the boys, chose you as the top student," Theopolus said.

"Thank you, sir."

"Genitos, it is obvious that you taught the boy the skills to accomplish such a feat. I remember you as a boy. You were the most athletic student, enabling your Greek school to soundly defeat the Romulus team. I know it is you! I would like to find out why you are a slave, but time is short. You and Eronte must leave today. Graduation tomorrow is for students and parents only. You are a slave and the boy a Jew. That is all."

Both Genitos and Eronte wore shocked expressions. With shoulders slumped, they stared at the proctor, unable to speak. Genitos shook with indignation, but as a slave he dared not speak his anger.

"One more thing, Eronte," Theopolus added. "The slave educator and the boys want you to have these two objects to remind you of them: a discus and a spear. You must leave as soon as possible."

Picking up the discus and spear, Eronte and Genitos left the office, feet dragging and faces downcast.

"Eronte, I will always remember you," they overheard Theopolus say. "You were the brightest and most dedicated student, and Genitos the most skilled coach to the top student ever at Romulus."

Silently, they questioned why then Eronte had been treated so harshly.

Over the four years of intensive training, Eronte had developed into a tall, handsome young man who was mentally and spiritually superior, yet humble.

With hasty preparation and their bags packed, they travelled quickly to the Roman harbour to locate a ship. As this chapter of Eronte's life closed, he and Genitos sailed across the Mediterranean back home to Jerusalem—and Emontial.

TWELVE

Homeward Bound

The chariot arriving from the port of Asquelon stopped in front of Emontial's house. Sitting on his porch, Emontial wondered who was coming to visit. A tall, handsome, well-built young man stepped down from the chariot and walked nobly toward the house.

Could this be Eronte, the boy who left four years ago? Emontial thought. He rushed off the porch to greet the tall stranger.

Eronte quickened his pace when he saw his beloved benefactor. "Emontial, I'm home! I'm home!"

They fell into each other's arms and hugged for what seemed an eternity.

"Is this the little man who left me four years ago?" Emontial stretched back to arm's length while continuing to hold Eronte's shoulders. "Let me have a good look at you!"

Genitos stood very proudly beside his protégé, whom he had guided, protected, and helped for four years. He then quietly slipped away as the two reconnected after four years of absence.

"Why are you here so soon?" Emontial asked. "I thought you would be much longer."

"Because I'm Jewish and Genitos a slave, we were not allowed to attend the final ceremonies."

"What? Because you are a Jew! And he a slave! I paid Theopolus double what the other parents paid, yet you were treated so poorly. When I go to Rome, I shall certainly speak to him. Let's not talk about that now. I'm so happy to see you."

"The slave teacher and the boys gave me a discus and spear with the Romulus crest so I would remember them and my days at Romulus," Eronte said. "The first months, I was so unhappy and lonely. The slave teacher beat me and the boys ridiculed me, but Genitos said I couldn't disappoint you, so I held my chest high and worked hard. I'm proud to tell you that Genitos guided me so well; I became the top student in all studies and sports."

They walked, talked, laughed, and contemplated the future. They discussed how Eronte would help Emontial become a better man, as he had promised years ago.

The happy greeting broke up as Eronte left to arrange his room.

Searching out Genitos, Emontial grabbed his slave's hand and hugged him. "I promised that if you guided the boy and he was successful, I would reward you. The positive influence you had on Eronte is obvious. Therefore, I set you free. You are no longer a slave. You are now the manager of all my businesses. For that honour, you will teach Eronte to be my successor by continuing as his top advisor. Under your tutelage, he will be capable of carrying on my legacy."

With emotion clouding his eyes, and his voice cracking, Genitos gave a deep bow. "Thank you, Emontial. I will continue to serve you."

As Genitos left, Emontial found himself alone in the garden. He contemplated how he had obtained his former prized slave, how he and Convictus, the two wealthiest businessmen in Jerusalem, had battled at the slave market to buy the best slaves for their enterprises.

Emontial had bought strong men to lift heavy iron at the chariot factory, skilled seamstresses to sew clothes at the apparel factory, and short, muscular men to work his quarry. Convictus had bought tall, handsome men to sell expensive clothes in his upscale clothing shops, beautiful well-figured women for his exclusive ladies wear establishments, and young pretty girls to model his original clothing to the elite.

It had been a contest for them to outbid other slave owners. Often they tried to outbid each other. They had fought bitterly over the prized, intelligent slave called Genitos.

"I bid five hundred for the slave Genitos!"

"I'll go one thousand!" Emontial had answered.

Very quickly Convictus came back with "Fifteen hundred."

Without hesitation, Emontial had bid, "Two thousand!"

With palpable anger, Convictus had growled, "Twenty-five hundred!"

Emontial had looked at Convictus and with a wry grin said, "He looks good enough to me. I'll top the bid to sixty-five hundred."

"What? No slave is worth that! Emontial, what are you doing? That one was to be mine to drive my chariots. I will never forget you stole him from me. Or forgive you! Watch out, Emontial, you slave stealer!"

And Convictus had stomped off.

THIRTEEN

Realization

After seeing Eronte settled, Emontial went to Convictus' menswear shop, looking for a gift to welcome his adopted son home. As he entered the building, he happened to see Convictus standing at the door.

"Are you here to give me Genitos, the slave you stole from me?" Convictus asked.

"No! Genitos isn't a slave anymore. I have released him. He's manager of the chariot plant. Business is booming. We just got an order from Rome for one thousand fast-tracking chariots."

"You did what? You will have to pay him a huge salary!"

"He deserves every shekel. With his ability to manage, I know chariot sales will quadruple. Genitos, having been a slave himself, knows how to make the slave workers happier and more productive. Having driven chariots in war, he will be able to design the exact chariots the Roman military needs to enforce their laws across the empire."

Convictus pumped his fist at Emontial. Without another word, he turned and stomped off.

Emontial shook his head. "I can't believe you are walking away!"

But the man had already gone. He sighed. *Convictus hasn't changed. He's still rude. I hope he isn't thinking about revenge of some sort. I feel sorry for him!*

Convictus had hurt many innocent people by forcing them into debt to make them slaves, and killing people for not obeying his commands. He took malicious pleasure in sending older slaves to Rome to entertain the Emperor in the Coliseum.

Emontial walked into the shop to buy a gift for Eronte. As he examined the clothing, he was greeted by a slave. He was tall, extremely handsome, and had a captivating smile. The man surprised Emontial with his intelligent language, carriage of body, and proper manners towards customers. The way this man handled himself, he obviously hadn't been born a slave.

"Are you the manager?" Emontial asked.

"Yes, I am Paulus, the shop manager."

"I'm here to buy a welcome home gift for my adoptive son. What would you suggest?"

"Come over here and see these gifts."

Emontial, studying the man's visage, was stunned to realize that his face was the mirror image of Eronte's. Could this be Eronte's father?

Paulus picked up a colourful robe and hastily handed it to him. Emontial quickly paid and then rushed out the door. Emontial couldn't concentrate; his mind was a whirl. Frightening thoughts passed through his mind.

Rushing out of the shop, Emontial headed home. He knew that Convictus had enslaved at least one husband and wife for a debt they owed.

Could it be true that this man and his wife were Eronte's father and mother? According to the Roman law, every child born of a slave woman was automatically a slave and belonged to the mother's slave owner. So if Paulus and his wife had been enslaved to Convictus, Eronte would belong to Convictus too.

For guiding, protecting, and treating Eronte like a free man, Convictus would charge me for stealing his slave, Emontial thought. *My punishment would be severe. All of my holdings would belong to Convictus, and I would also become his slave.*

"What if my fears are true?" he whispered to himself. "What can I do to save Eronte and myself from slavery? And Genitos and my factory workers!"

If Convictus learned about this, he would thoroughly enjoy administering on them the harshest punishment under Roman law.

Arriving home, Emontial urgently located Eronte and Genitos.

"I have a pressing matter to be dealt with near Rome," Emontial said. "I need you both to speedily build a factory on the water and build war chariots to fulfill my orders. My competition must not know I am building a new factory outside Rome. You must leave within the hour. Travel directly to Asquelon, board my galley, and sail for Rome."

"Yes," Genitos said. "Eronte and I will do as you instruct, sir."

"Listen carefully: it is crucial that you do not stop en route to converse with anyone as you journey to Asquelon. Do not ask any questions. Do not contact me. All must be done in secret. I will contact you. Use all the resources you need. Pack with haste and go!"

FOURTEEN

The Bet

After rushing them out the door, Emontial breathed heavily and headed back to the shops district. He entered another of Convictus' stores, this one for ladies wear.

Hurry, Emontial! Think! Think! He spotted the slave manager of the shop. When he saw her, he realized she was extremely beautiful. She stood erect, serving many customers in her charming way. She seemed more like a princess than a slave. Her carriage and manner of addressing the customers indicated that she, like Paulus, hadn't always been enslaved.

"I must find out more about her," he murmured under his breath. He furrowed his brow. "Could she be Eronte's mother?"

He spoke with her for a few moments, and she said that her name was Marlan. He thanked her and hurried out of the shop.

On his way to his chariot, Emontial recalled a bet he and Convictus had made twenty-five years ago.

That's it, he thought, smiling. *I know what to do!*

He immediately strode to Convictus' office, marched in, and sat down without an invitation.

"Remember when we journeyed to Rome?" Emontial asked. "We really enjoyed the races at Circus Maximus."

Convictus' only reaction was to stare coldly into Emontial's eyes. Though he used no words, Emontial knew the man was dismissing him.

Emontial ignored the dismissive attitude and banged his fist on the table for emphasis. "Convictus, I'd like to take you for dinner. Anywhere you choose, and I'll pay the bill no matter what it costs. Let us put an end to this quarrelling."

Convictus continued to glare at Emontial in his vicious way, and stood up. "All right! We'll go immediately."

He led Emontial to the city's most exclusive eating establishment, one that Convictus himself owned.

With a conniving smile, Convictus ordered two of the most expensive meals served. "We will begin with breads and oil to dip the bread, and bring us a serving bowl of fruit. We will have a platter of fish later. But first, I'll order the best imported wine from Rome."

Convictus instructed the server to leave the food until they had time to consume several glasses of this very expensive wine. Convictus purposely had the wine poured into oversized glasses and swirled it to observe the colour.

"Drink up!" Convictus said. "Since you invited me, and I own this fine establishment, I'm having you charged the top price for everything served during this dinner."

"You are my guest. Please, enjoy yourself. Let us raise our glasses and drink them to the last drop. Try to remember, Convictus, at least for a little while, the great friends we used to be."

Each man, consumed by his own thoughts, drank his wine to the bottom of the glass without taking a breath.

Emontial grabbed a second bottle of wine and poured each glass to the top. "Shall we make another toast and drink these to the bottom?"

"Certainly. I'll toast that the more this dinner costs you, the more enjoyment I'll get out of being here. It just goes to show how foolish a man you are."

"Drink up, Convictus! We will see who the better man is."

They both drank to the bottom and Convictus reached for another bottle, refilling the glasses. Both men conversed loudly, showing their level of intoxication.

"Convictus, twenty-five years ago, you and I sat in these same seats, drank heavily, ate a good meal, and made a bet. Do you remember?"

"What? Twenty-five years ago! No, my memory is absent on that occasion. What are you going on about?"

"You and I made a bet about who would be the most successful businessman. We even put the bet on paper and had it legally stamped. The judgment was to be based on who purchased and owned the most slaves over the next twenty-five years. The winner was to have the privilege of choosing one slave from all those that the loser owned. The loser must give up the chosen slave. Today is the day for this debt to be paid."

"Ah ha! I have obviously won. I own more slaves than you, you fool. Drink up. Celebrate with me. I will claim the slave Genitos, the one you stole from me, and he will proudly drive me around in my prize chariot. Go! Get the legal document, Emontial. Get out of here!"

As Emontial stumbled toward the door for home, he heard Convictus add with a sneer, "Ha! Speedily return with the legal document to prove I am the winner! You fool. Genitos will be mine."

Emontial took a deep breath, turned about, and steadied himself. "Yes, I will fetch the document and return with haste," he said in a voice dripping with honey. "You know, we drank quite a bit. Would you like to wait until we are sober tomorrow?"

"No! Definitely not! I will claim Genitos today. I know that I've won. I am the winner!"

"Very well then. Send for Tribune Narcellus. He will make the proper legal decision."

"Consider it done!"

FIFTEEN

The Bet, Part II

Emontial walked slowly, taking each step carefully due to his alcohol consumption. He smiled wryly as he climbed into his chariot to travel home, confident that his plan was working.

Once home, he headed to the private room where he kept his valuables. He unlatched the chest door directly under the desk, reached into the back, and retrieved the twenty-five-year-old papyrus scroll describing their agreement. He rolled the scroll tightly and placed it carefully in the large pocket of his robe.

Emontial sighed with relief. This agreement would ensure that he could claim Marlan.

He then returned to Convictus at the dining establishment. Tribune Narcellus sat with him, impatient to see this agreement that meant so much to Convictus, who was becoming more inebriated.

"Open it! Open it!" Convictus yelled. "I have won! Give me Genitos! He's my slave!"

Emontial reached into his robe, withdrew the scroll, and placed it on the table in front of Narcellus. Narcellus picked up the scroll, unrolled it, and verified its age. Then he began to read aloud so both Convictus and Emontial could hear: "The one of us who buys the most slaves over the next twenty-five years from this day will be given the opportunity to choose one slave in the other's possession and claim that slave as his own."

The document was signed by Emontial and Convictus and legally executed.

Tribune Narcellus verified that the signatures were authentic.

Convictus, stumbling to his feet, screamed in a drunken stupor, "I won! Bring me Genitos so that I may choose my prize. Because he is your slave, I will work him 'til he dies. Ha! I will have my revenge for the way you cheated me."

"Just wait a minute, Convictus!" Emontial said. "Not so fast. Narcellus must make an appointment at the slavery office to be given the official records. These records state in detail the role each of us has played in the past twenty-five years dealing with slaves."

The tribune agreed, stood up, and announced, "Yes, Emontial speaks correctly. I will not take you to the office today, because you are both inebriated. Tomorrow morning, at sunrise, legionnaires will escort you officially to the slavery building. The facts of this situation need to be reviewed from the director's records. My judgment will be final." Saluting both men, with a hand held to his heart, Tribune Narcellus stood at attention. "Good night, gentlemen!"

He left quickly.

Losing control, Convictus screamed, "Let's have another glassful to celebrate my victory."

Emontial answered in a whisper, "See you tomorrow morning."

As he headed home, Emontial smiled, thinking to himself how easy a victory he would have tomorrow. Eronte, Genitos, and he would be saved. He had caused Convictus to become drunk on purpose, hoping he would not realize what the contract actually said.

Part one of my plan is well laid.

SIXTEEN

Court Decision

Early the next morning, five minutes apart, Convictus and Emontial arrived by chariot at the slavery office. Escorted by legionnaires to the courtroom where slave disputes were decided, they waited in complete silence, sitting on stone benches on either each side of the courtroom. Only one would be the victor, but both expected they would win. Their lightened moods warmed the dull grey of the courtroom walls.

The massive wooden door behind the tribune's bench opened, and out stepped a colourfully dressed legionnaire. He marched to the centre of the room, between the two men, and stood at attention. He ordered everyone to stand. Narcellus, attired in a flowing purple robe, entered majestically and proceeded to the high chair, followed by the slavery official who sat at a lower level.

"Based on the legal contract in my hands, the final judgment will be decided for one of you to release to the other a slave of his choice. The winner may choose one slave from all the slaves that the loser owns. Slavery official, stand and read aloud to the court the legal records which contain the slavery dealings each man handled over the past twenty-five years."

"Tribune Narcellus, the records show that Convictus, over the past twenty-five years, dealt with slaves in the following ways: received as gifts, 76; born to his female slaves, 571; purchased at auction, 2,552. The total of all slaves officially dealt with, 3,199.

"Emontial, over the past twenty-five years, dealt with slaves in the following ways: received as gifts, 33; born to his female slaves, 43; purchased at auction, 2,641. The total of all slaves officially dealt with, 2,717."

Narcellus nodded. "Thank you for those official records. Court will be recessed until I return with my decision based on your legal document."

The legionnaire stood at attention and instructed everyone to rise. Narcellus rose, turned, and walked through the podium door with the slavery official following.

Both slave owners exited into the courtyard without saying a word to one another. Convictus had a cruel, sneering smile on his face. He tried to get his opponent to observe this smirk of satisfaction, knowing he was the victor because he had owned more slaves. Emontial, not wanting to give Convictus satisfaction, avoided the other's glance by looking around at the Roman architecture.

After what seemed an eternity, the legionnaire appeared and instructed them that Tribune Narcellus awaited. The opponents quickly returned to the courtroom to hear his decision.

Entering the courtroom, one man with a swagger and the other with calm confidence, the two men saw Narcellus already sitting at his raised bench, ready to declare his decision.

"Convictus, Emontial, come and stand before me."

Reaching the front of the court, the two men were separated by a pair of burly legionnaires. The men looked up at Narcellus with expectancy, anticipating his decision.

"The legal document you both signed states that the person who bought the most slaves over the next twenty-five years would be the winner. Bought means to pay money. The auction sells slaves for money paid in cash. Therefore, it is irrelevant to base my decision on the total number of slaves dealt with because that includes slaves received as gifts and slaves born of female slaves. The gifted and born slaves do not qualify as bought."

Convictus' eyes widened as he stared at Narcellus in disgust with the realization that his opponent would win. Emontial smiled widely.

"Convictus, you bought 2,552 slaves from the auction over the past twenty-five years," Narcellus continued. "Emontial, you bought 2,641 slaves from the auction over the past twenty-five years. Therefore, my decision, effective immediately: you two adversaries will be escorted by myself and four legionnaires to Convictus' main office. There he will be required to give up one slave of Emontial's choosing. As a result, Emontial, you have the right to choose one slave to be yours from the entire number of slaves owned by Convictus."

The two men, one joyful, the other seething with anger, were surrounded by legionnaires and escorted with haste to Convictus' office.

"Emontial, choose your slave quickly now," said Narcellus. "My soldiers and I can escort you and your slave safely to your property. Your opponent is obviously upset with my decision, and I do want these events to end peacefully. Which slave do you choose?"

"The beautiful female slave who sells clothes in the ladies clothing shop."

"She is yours. Legionnaires, bring the specified slave here."

Two legionnaires left and returned shortly with the clothing shop slave.

"Is she the slave you are claiming, Emontial?" Narcellus asked.

Emontial measured his words carefully despite a voice full of emotion. "Yes, that is she!"

The legionnaires escorted them to the waiting chariot.

In the chariot on the way home, Emontial said to her, "I remember speaking with you at the ladies shop. Your name is Marlan. Is that right?

"Yes, that's correct. Marlan is my name."

"You managed the ladies wear shop for Convictus. Obviously you must be able to read, write, and do financial numbers."

Marlan looked bewildered but sensed the respectful attitude of this slave owner. "Thank you, sir," she said cautiously. "Yes, I can."

"As my slave, you will supervise all the other slaves. You will not cook or clean, but I would like you to do the marketing, answer the door, and manage the entire household."

Stunned, she could only stare at Emontial. "I will try to do as you command."

But why me? she asked herself.

Sensing that Marlan was the mother of Eronte, Emontial knew the best plan would be to leave the matter of their relationship for a later time. He could only hope it wasn't true.

Once again the horror of his dilemma surfaced. If he found out for certain that Marlan was Eronte's mother, and if he freed Marlan right now, would Eronte be a free man and thus save Emontial and his holdings from Convictus? If that vindictive man found out Eronte was a slave hidden from him while Marlan was a slave, Convictus would take everything Emontial owned with the greatest vindictive pleasure and take Emontial as a slave. Clearly, Convictus wanted to torture him in every way, mentally and physically, even to death.

To distract himself from these worries, Emontial showed Marlan through his house and specifically stated her duties. It was entirely new for her to be treated in such a respectful way.

Again she wondered, *Why? How nice it would be to have my husband working as a slave for Emontial.*

SEVENTEEN

Revenge

Convictus, still seething with anger at his loss, screamed and howled in rage. "I will personally destroy Emontial's world! I'll gain revenge for this blow to my pride! That man stole my most prized slave, Genitos, and now Marlan!"

He grabbed a full pitcher of wine and guzzled it without stopping for breath. Then he refilled the pitcher to the top and drank it. Reeling drunk, he downed a third pitcher and fell comatose on the floor.

Early the following morning, he found himself still sprawled on the floor and suffering from a throbbing headache. Convictus picked himself off the floor and wobbled to his bathhouse, where he spent most of the day recovering and planning tactics to gain total revenge. Eight days later, his plans were completed. He would ensure that Emontial personally returned his favourite female slave.

Thus, on the tenth day after the tribune's decision, Convictus walked determinedly to Emontial's home, revising in his mind the revengeful, ruinous plans.

He banged on the door, each hit more thunderous than the previous one. "Emontial, open this door! I'm here to talk to you!"

Surprised yet concerned, Emontial greeted the man cordially. "Good afternoon, Convictus. What brings you out to visit? Come, sit with me on the porch in the sun and empty a rich glass of my finest wine."

Convictus falsely apologized for his past behaviour. "I value our friendship over the past many years. We've had some happy and exciting adventures together."

"Yes, we certainly have!"

The conversation between the two became pleasant yet guarded on Emontial's part. He remained suspiciously optimistic while Convictus rambled on.

They reminisced about old times when they had travelled together, sailed together, and rode in chariots together. They had helped each other succeed with underhanded deals in the business world. Anyone listening to them and their tall tales would have thought they were the best of friends and always thought well of each other.

Convictus reminded Emontial about their play-filled days in Rome, when they took time off from business dealings to converse in the most expensive seats at Circus Maximus, experiencing the spectacular sport of chariot racing.

Emontial clapped his hands in glee and laughed heartily. "Watching those chariot races was one of the best times of our friendship."

Sensing his plan coming to fruition, Convictus turned his face away to stifle a sneer. "Yes, chariot racing was the most enjoyable event to attend in Rome." He reached for another glass of wine. "Remember our joy-filled days at the track, surrounded by a hundred thousand spectators? Unbelievable!"

"Yes, Convictus." Emontial remembered those days well. The sandy oval circuit had made it impossible to have individual racing lanes. Few rules had existed. The average driver had a relatively short career, ending in injury or—more often—death.

"The excitement of watching such catastrophic crashes! Mangled bodies! Chariots overturned! Horses piled in heaps!"

Emontial felt disgust at Convictus' bloodlust as he recalled those days at Circus Maximus. The first racing team to complete seven rounds had always been the winner. An ordinary race day had held ten to twelve races, but a major event had held twenty-four. The spectators had treated the drivers as great heroes, even though most charioteers were slaves. These slaves had earned huge amounts of money. If they lived long enough, they could buy their way out of slavery.

"I always visited the stables to pick out my favourite team, and get racing tips from the charioteers," Convictus said.

The teams of horses were called an Auriga, and the most experienced and muscular horse, the funalis, had always raced on the left.

"And you did get some good money-making tips, if I remember correctly," Emontial said "As you know, one of my most important businesses is my chariot factory. The best chariots are small and lightweight, built of wood, and offer no protection or support for the driver. The charioteer must balance himself on the axle while racing seven times around the spina."

After finishing their guarded conversation, Convictus smiled. "Let's meet again soon. We'll talk about the possibility of returning to Rome and watch the chariot races. Goodbye for now, Emontial."

Convictus turned and gritted his teeth, his facial features becoming frightful.

The first part of my plan was successful, he thought.

Meanwhile, Emontial contemplated traveling to Rome. *It will give me an opportunity, without Convictus knowing, to see Eronte and Genitos again, and further my plans.*

EIGHTEEN

Messages and Plans

A herald from Eronte entered Emontial's private office. When instructed, he closed the door and stood at attention in front of Emontial's substantial wooden desk, waiting for the order to repeat the personal message Eronte had sent.

The herald, a well-educated slave, had the ability to memorize in detail a message exactly as it was dictated. There was therefore no security risk, for the message wasn't written down.

"Speak," ordered Emontial.

"A message from Eronte," the herald began. "Have located six acres for sale on the southern plain of Campania overlooking an excellent harbour. Negotiating lowest price for the purchase of this property. Materials needed to build the plant and manufacture the product are available at reasonable rates. Construction team, whether slaves or workers, are readily available. Hope this message is satisfactory. Waiting for your reply. Regards, Eronte."

Feeling proud of his protégé, Emontial smiled and ordered the herald to dictate a return message: "Message from Emontial to Eronte. Excellent report. Coming to Rome with Convictus to see once again Circus Maximus. Date unknown. It is essential we meet in secret. I will find you. I will be disguised. Will explain in detail when I see you in person. Do not repeat this message. I repeat: do not, under any circumstance, reveal this information to anyone."

Emontial waited impatiently for Convictus to visit once again, which he was certain would happen. It could not happen soon enough.

That very afternoon, Convictus dropped in unannounced. With a conniving smile, he said, "If you want to go to Circus Maximus, I will arrange our travelling plans. I'll pay for everything!"

Emontial stared at Convictus as if in complete surprise. “I’m shocked at the rush you’re in. Maybe we should wait and think about this for a while. To me, it’s too hurried. Sit down and share a glass of wine with me. Let’s discuss how to organize this trip, if we do decide to travel.”

A momentary flash of anger creased Convictus’ eyes, but his expression quickly transformed into a wide smile. “This trip will take at least a month to organize. Emontial, I owe you an apology for the way I treated you. I’ll be responsible for our passage. We’ll use a sailing vessel and stay at the Dolce, the finest inn near the racetrack. And I intend to rent the most expensive Circus Maximus box, situated at the finish line.”

Emontial raised his glass, not wanting to appear eager. “Well, Convictus, you’re a very convincing man. Yes, of course I accept your offer.”

“Well then, let us toast this interesting endeavour.” Their glasses raised and clinked. “To Rome, to horse racing, to new adventures.”

“To our renewed friendship!” Emontial said. “Drink one more glass of wine, then go home and make this dream come true. I’ll be ready to travel immediately. The sooner the better.”

Convictus returned to his office by chariot. *I’ve succeeded in the next part of my vengeful plan,* he thought.

Once alone, Emontial felt deeply satisfied. His deception had misled Convictus for the moment.

He hoped he could achieve freedom for himself and Eronte, yet confused thoughts still invaded his mind. Even though he had Marlan in his employ, could Convictus still lay claim to Eronte, as he had helped the boy when Marlan was Convictus’ slave?

* * *

A month to the day of their agreement, Convictus arrived at Emontial’s home and the two men journeyed to Asquelon to catch their ship, the *Argus*. Travelling in ideal weather, the ship arrived without incident at Rome, where they were transported in slave-shouldered padded chairs to the Dolce. They were treated like senators with the most luxurious suites, the innkeeper’s tastiest food, and the finest imported wine.

Both men handled each other with false respect as they ended a pleasure-filled day by looking across the great city. The setting sun lit the porticos at the Roman Forum, shining on the marble of the government building surrounding the plaza.

"Convictus, look," Emontial said, pointing. "Look out there at the Coliseum. It hasn't changed in all the years we've been away. A toast! I toast this great city, our renewed friendship, and you, Convictus, for making this dream a reality."

"I drink to that!" Convictus looked at the plaza below. "I made many offhanded business deals in this plaza."

Stifling a yawn, Emontial stretched. "I am weary. What are our plans for tomorrow?"

"First we breakfast on fruits and breads. Then we'll go to Circus Maximus to watch the opening parade march by our VIP box."

"All right, off to bed. Good night, Convictus."

"Good night. Tomorrow will be an eventful day."

More eventful than you realize, Convictus thought with a sly smile. *When my plans materialize, you and all you own will be mine.*

They dragged themselves to bed, each contemplating their next moves.

NINETEEN

Spectacle and Stealth

After breakfast, they arrived on time to view the spectacular parade, legionnaires marching militarily, drummers sounding like thunder, trumpets screeching, clowns cavorting, followed by the chariots speeding over the sandy track, driven by champion drivers. Convictus and Emontial toasted the entire parade with the best wine served.

After the parade, they separated to go about personal business.

"Emontial, I'm going straight to the stables to learn the tips for today's races," Convictus said. "I'll inquire what it would cost to hire a driver, horses, and chariot to cross the Mediterranean. It would be a smart deal to hold races in Jerusalem."

Convictus knew he could be upfront with his dealings. It would be seen as normal to try bringing races to his hometown. Inwardly, however, he had an ulterior motive that would ruin his so-called friend.

"Emontial, let's meet back here at midafternoon."

"Yes, Convictus. That will be fine."

Both men were aware that the other would be followed throughout the day by spies.

Emontial went straight to a doctor's office, walked in, and looked through the window to check if the spy had seen him enter.

He greeted the doctor warmly, as a very old friend. "A spy followed me and I have personal business I must attend to. Do you have any old clothes I can use?"

"I have just the disguise you require." The doctor produced a sea captain's garb complete with false beard, white jacket with shoulder pad stripes, and a captain's triangular cap.

With a hearty thank you, Emontial disguised himself and eased out the back door. *Now, to find Eronte and Genitos.*

Locating them at his newly constructed factory, Emontial explained that the secrecy of his visit was crucial.

"Genitos, Convictus wanted you more than any other slave," Emontial said. "You are tall, good looking, well-educated, and most importantly a soldier able to drive his personal chariot. Because I bid more than twice as much as he did, he accused me of stealing you. He was furious. At the moment, Convictus appears to be happy. I wish to keep him that way, so neither of you must ever come to me." He took a deep breath and changed the subject. "I spoke with a man at the inn who owns a small factory making racing chariots for Circus Maximus. I plan to buy this factory and use it as an experimental site to have you develop a cart that races faster than any built before. I'll contact you when all is ready to begin. I'm off now. Remember, only I will contact you."

Emontial retraced his steps to the doctor's back door, entered, changed his clothing, and exited out the front. He knew that the spy watching his moves would have something suitable to report to his owner; if the spy had lost him and had nothing to say, Convictus would have the slave executed.

Now I'm ready to face Convictus, he thought.

TWENTY

White Arabians and Races

Entering their prized box at the stadium, Emontial noticed an Arabian man seated in the parallel box. He looked like royalty, the centre of attention, and was treated like a king by all surrounding him. Since he was waiting for Convictus to arrive from the stables, he smiled and spoke to the man.

"Good day, sir. I trust you enjoyed the parade. Do you have any teams racing today?"

Thus Emontial met Sheik Ostis al-Hussein.

"No, I don't, but I own many white Arabians that would soundly defeat any of those racing today." Al-Hussein described his white stallions in detail, emphasizing the physical features that enabled them to be the strongest and fastest—horses that could never lose. "My stallions have a short back and a long, arched neck, running well back into the high withers. The croup is horizontal, the chest deep, the legs strong and dense, and the ribs well sprung. A finely formed head holds a very attractive face. The tail is carried so high that, viewed from the rear, it looks to be straight. The horses have large nostrils which, when extended, reveal blood vessels emanating from their small muzzles. This enables the stallions to breathe with ease when racing. Their muscled hindquarters make it possible to be agile, have intense bursts of activity, and have the stamina necessary for endurance. The hooves have dense, strong hoof walls. My stallions are also affectionate and love to be petted. I never hit or strike them with a whip or a stick."

"You are obviously proud of your racing stallions," Emontial remarked.

"Yes. They are the most magnificent breed of horse for racing," al-Hussein said. "I am Ostis al-Hussein and I live in North Africa where I camp at Ziz Oasis with my wives, my white Arabians, my training grounds, and my servants."

"It is a distinct pleasure to meet you, sir! My name is Emontial and I'm a businessman from Jerusalem. I own a chariot factory in Rome. In fact, right now I'm having a chariot experimentally designed that will be the fastest lightweight racing chariot."

"Really! Interesting! Well, this is a chance meeting! Good to meet you. Since you've shown such interest in my horses, it would be my pleasure to have you as a guest in my home anytime you wish to visit. Perhaps we could combine your experimental chariot with my Arabians to make a superior racing team."

Emontial smiled at the man. "Thank you for your kind invitation. When my chariots are developed, I just might have need of supreme racers."

Just then, Convictus arrived. "Emontial, I have learned the greatest tips," he said. "I'm going to make money today. I intend to enjoy several glasses of the finest Roman wine."

The sheik gave Convictus a quick sideways glance. He raised his eyebrows, then turned his attention to watch the race preparations.

The box Emontial and Convictus had rented was situated next to the highest official's imperial box. Sometimes the Emperor himself watched the parade from there.

The opening procession showcased each team accompanied by their standards, many musicians, attending magistrates, and the circus workers. They all entered through the Porta Triumphal.

The dignitaries seated themselves in the imperial box and signalled the races to begin. Immediately the chariots and their famous drivers entered from the stables, called carceres, to the sound of blaring trumpets. Circus Maximus seated 150,000 attendees and was composed of two long parallel sides, one end rounded and filled with seats with the other end containing stables and starting gates. A wall, or spina, occupied the centre of the track, surrounded by imposing architecture.

A maximum of twelve chariots competed, racing seven laps for each race. Speed determined the winner. Chariots were very light, and thus structurally weak. The drivers, standing on a single axle, could be tossed from their chariot and trampled by charging horses, twisted to death in the wreckage, or tangled in the reins and cruelly dragged to their deaths. Convictus found the carnage exhilarating, the more gore the better, while Emontial disliked the suffering.

After drinking two full glasses of wine, Convictus remarked, "Remember, there are four teams each with a different colour: white, blue, green, or red. Pick your colour."

"White!" Emontial said.

"I pick red. Now, let's bet one thousand denarii on each of the twelve races, payable at the end of the day over a glass of the best wine when we return to our lodgings at the Dolce."

"Sounds like fun! I agree. Good luck!"

The head magistrate in the imperial box dropped the mappa cloth to start the race.

"Convictus, look!" Emontial said. "The white team is in front, and the red is last."

"Restrain yourself, Emontial. There are seven laps all together. I know I'll win!"

White won that first race. Convictus, drinking heavily, became stonily silent as he reflected on how to gain his revenge.

When the twelfth race finished, Emontial had won one more than Convictus. Hastening to their lodgings, Convictus filled their wine glasses to the top with a twisted smile and reluctantly paid Emontial the one thousand denarii.

"Well, Emontial, you won today. Yes, you are the victor, but don't gloat; there is still tomorrow."

Both drank considerably and then struggled off to bed.

* * *

After breakfast the next morning, the two men retraced their steps to the ship and sat on the deck in companionable conversation munching on grapes, figs, and breads dripping with oil. As was customary, they consumed further glasses of wine.

Convictus guided the discussion toward the popularity of horse racing. "Emontial, think about yesterday. Horse racing is so popular. The pomp and ceremony, the dignitaries, the thousands of people, the money exchanged... yes, and all the money to be made! We could make money by sponsoring chariot races close to Jerusalem."

"Hmm! Sponsoring chariot races. That might be an interesting venture to explore. Yes, an interesting venture indeed."

The *Argus* sailed quietly across the Mediterranean to Asquelon. Both men sat in quiet thought, listening to the slap of the waves on the side of the boat.

Convictus oozed evil from every pore with his thoughts of revenge. He spent many hours contemplating his next move. With his back turned to Emontial, he wandered the deck to look over the stern of the ship.

How can I win back Marlan? he wondered. *What can I do to make Emontial suffer? He seems to be interested in the sport of racing. Maybe something regarding racing!* He paused, a smile crossing his face. *I've got it!*

Emontial's thoughts, on the other hand, were based on ways to free him from his fears of losing everything. He knew that Convictus, if given the chance, would destroy his world emotionally, physically, and revengefully with swiftness so complete that his freemen, workers, slaves, and businesses would be devastated. The more chaos and destruction he caused, the happier Convictus would be. All that Emontial had accomplished in his life would be obliterated.

How could he stop Convictus from ruining his life? What could Emontial do to make his dreams come true? How could he use his resources to ensure that those he loved were safe? He yearned for Eronte to be free, the boy who had started him on this journey from misery and cruelty by caring for him and touching him with the sandals of Jesus. Emontial had been freed with Christ's power to become a new man.

Emontial knew the strict Roman law. If he stole a slave, or hid or kept a stolen slave, all his possessions would be confiscated by the rightful owner. He would subsequently become that owner's slave. The legal question would be whether Eronte was a slave owned by Convictus. If so, Emontial was in serious trouble. But if Marlan was Eronte's mother, and if he freed her, would the courts deem her child free also? It all depended on the interpretation of the law.

Emontial wandered the decks, still deep in thought. *I know that the law reads, "Children of female slaves are automatically slaves." But Eronte was never in actual slavery; he worked in that fruit and vegetable market stall before he was given the sandals of Jesus. If this came to trial at the slavery court, what would be the ruling?*

The *Argus* arrived at the port of Asquelon. With hasty goodbyes, both men parted, eager to go their own way.

TWENTY-ONE

Brilliant Scheme

Two weeks later, very early in the morning, Convictus charged onto Emontial's porch. "Come out here, Emontial!" he yelled. "We have business to discuss. I've thought it out. People will enjoy the races. We'll make money. We'll both make piles of money!"

Emontial stumbled onto the porch. "What is it you want? I'm still half asleep. The sun hasn't even risen!"

"Listen to me. You know, we've never been able to do anything profitable with our scrubland outside of town. We can use it for a racing stadium. We'll make money, all kinds of it! It's a brilliant scheme to gain us more fame than ever before. We're great now, but we will be greater!"

"I'm not sure, Convictus. Let me think. Perhaps we could construct a temporary stadium based on the Circus Maximus model with wooden stands. Maybe you're right."

"I know I'm right. It would be built cheaply, but with enough decoration to attract up to a hundred thousand patrons. We could even bring one of the Maximus hero charioteers to drive in the opening race. Imagine all the money from food concessions, and the rich parading around in my expensive robes. Think of all the toy chariots, the javelins, shields, and other military equipment you could sell. Come here. Look at my plans. Look at them! Let's start immediately!"

They both sat and discussed the project.

Emontial ordered their customary wine and continued with false praise. "Convictus, you're so wound up! Calm yourself. Where in that scrubland would you construct the track?"

"In the middle of the field, to enable people in attendance to park their carts and horses around the outside. Just imagine it, Emontial! I want to make money. And I repeat: I know we can make a great deal of money. We'll not only be the richest men in Jerusalem, but in the whole Roman Empire."

"You are convincing, Convictus."

The deal was soon sealed.

* * *

Convictus and Emontial immediately commenced fulfilling these challenging plans, splitting expenses right down the middle. Construction began in the centre of the field. The stadium had the same measurements as Circus Maximus, seven thousand paces long and 133 paces wide. The base of the track was made of sand and contained no lanes for the horses to run in.

A walled brick barrier, the spina, was constructed to stretch the length of the inside track, making it difficult, almost impossible, to turn the horses around the ends. The turning posts at each end of the spina, called metae, contained three immovable stone pillars. Charioteers had to be hardened athletes strong enough to turn the horses tightly around each end of the spina. Often drivers rounding the sharp curve were crushed against these strong pillars, causing drivers and horses to crash into each other with chariots overturned and battered charioteers dragged along by wild horses. Many drivers were mangled, and many brutally killed. Spectators revelled in the carnage.

Several rows of seats rose up under canopied awnings and provided shade. They erected many shops, facing the countryside, for people to buy food, clothing, gifts, and toy chariots with horses and drivers.

The twelve wooden starting stalls were staggered to give each driver an even chance at the start of the race. Stalls were allocated by lottery. Seven colourful contoured balls, called eggs, were positioned atop the middle of the spina. One egg was removed after each lap to indicate to the excited crowd which lap had been completed.

As the stadium neared completion, Emontial and Convictus rode out to inspect their prize project. Satisfied with the progress, they returned to Convictus' office, relaxed, and had their usual celebratory wine. To allow time for all preparations, the first set of races were scheduled for harvest time. Nine races would be run the first day, because of the lengthy parade, the bands, the clowns, and the important elite. Maybe even the Emperor would attend.

Convictus always had vengeance on his mind. He stared at Emontial and spoke determinedly. "To start the festivities, you and I can race against each other for a valuable prize in the very first race."

"Sounds like a splendid idea. It would create more excitement with the spectators."

"Money doesn't matter to us, so we should bet a prize possession. Something which would affect us emotionally! Something we would not sell or give to anyone."

"Well, what do you suggest? What would be the prize?"

"You legally stole my slave, Marlan. Without her, my ladies wear business is gone. You will not sell her back to me for any price. If you bet Marlan, I'll bet her former husband, Paulus, the manager of the menswear shop, and I will include any other ten slaves you wish."

Without hesitation, Emontial reached out his hand. He knew he had a way to win this race. "Done!"

Convictus called in his scribe to legalize the agreed terms and witness both men signing to make the bet official. One man anticipated the relief of victory, and the other the sweetness of victorious revenge.

Both men filled their wine glasses to the top and joyfully danced around the room.

"Goodbye, Emontial. In the fall, all will be ready."

"Goodbye, Convictus."

As Emontial exited, he sensed his opponent's cold stare bristle the hairs on the back of his neck.

Quietly, Convictus added to himself, "Now to Rome to find some fast horses and a winning hero driver."

TWENTY-TWO

A Visit to Ziz

Emontial recalled Sheik Ostis al-Hussein's kind invitation and hastily prepared to set off for the Ziz Oasis in the Sahara Desert. Upon arriving at the sheik's camp, he was greeted royally.

"Welcome, Emontial. It is gratifying to see you again," said al-Hussein. "I'm so pleased you have come. Is this a visit regarding my horses?"

"Yes, thank you. I'm here to visit you and your majestic Arabian stallions. I remember that you said they could outrace all other horses with ease."

The sheik gave him a gigantic smile of approval. "You have an excellent memory. Come with me. I'll take you to see my best stallions."

They walked gracefully side by side, conversing comfortably, to a white tent emblazoned with gold. The flaps opened to show four stunning white Arabian stallions. The stallions lifted their heads, whinnied at the motion of the flaps, and trotted softly to the sheik. He quietly spoke to each by name, gently patting their necks. He treated them as if they were his sons. When he told them to greet Emontial, they lowered their heads.

Emontial reached out, patted them, and called their names just like al-Hussein had. They whinnied and stood proudly in line to show off their fantastic physiques.

"These are most impressive racing horses!" Emontial said. "Where do you train them?"

"My training area is beyond the far red tent. Let us sit in the shade for a moment with a cool drink to quench our thirst. Then I'll show you. Come, my friend. You have travelled a great distance to see me. I'm happy to see you, but you look concerned."

Startled at the sheik's awareness, Emontial spoke hesitantly but with honesty. "Yes, you have discerned correctly. I'm extremely worried."

"Tell me and my horses what is troubling you, and my horses and I will try to help. It's obvious that my Arabians trust you, Emontial, and they know what a person is really like on the inside. I discerned what a true man you are when I first met you. That's the only reason I invited you to my camp. Open up to us. Tell us your deepest concerns."

"Several years ago, when my slum tenants almost killed me, a young boy named Eronte saved my life by placing on my chest the sandals of Jesus Christ, a healer who had just been crucified by the Romans. A miracle happened. I instantly felt peace within myself. I realized how wonderful it was to be alive. I craved to learn more about the healer who had worn those sandals. As I studied and understood more of the teachings of Jesus Christ, my thoughts changed from wanting to see people suffer to wanting to help people with my heart, mind, and soul, to treat everyone as I would want to be treated. In time, I became a follower of Jesus, a Christian. My lifestyle changed completely."

"That is a wonderful revelation, my friend. Please, go on."

"I thanked the homeless lad by treating him like a son. I sent him to the best school in Rome, and I tried to find his parents because the lad didn't know where they were. One day when buying a new robe to welcome Eronte home from school, I visited a men's clothing shop in the upper market. To my amazement, I discovered Paulus, the slave who managed the shop for Convictus—and Eronte was the spitting image of this man!"

"What a shocking experience!"

"Yes, but that's not all. Convictus hates me, because through business dealings and bets, I won the manager of his ladies wear shop, Marlan. Convictus wants Marlan back, so he suggested that we bet on a chariot race at our newly built stadium. The winner will become the owner of both Marlan and Paulus. I strongly suspect they are, in fact, Eronte's parents. I agreed to the bet immediately, because if I won and freed them I could hopefully circumvent the strict Roman law which says that every child born of a slave woman is automatically a slave. It is necessary to free Marlan, but I would also free Paulus so all three could be a complete family again. It worries me to think what would happen if I lose. Not only would Eronte and his parents be Convictus' slaves, but I might lose everything for harbouring the child all these years."

The horses pawed the ground, pressing ears forward while al-Hussein stared into space, thinking deeply.

"This certainly is a frightening situation, Emontial," the sheik said. "We will help you win that race. Go to Rome, to Circus Maximus. In secret, hire the best driver. Return promptly with that charioteer, and I will train him with my best stallions. Good luck. May safe passage go with you on your quest."

* * *

Emontial travelled directly to Rome to see Eronte and Genitos. Meeting them at the chariot factory outside the city, he informed them of the race and the bet he had made with Convictus. Emontial purposely left out the fact that the two slaves they'd bet on were Eronte's suspected mother and father.

"You two are to design and build the lightest, strongest, fastest chariot," Emontial said. "I'm going to Circus Maximus to find Convictus and make him believe that I'm trying to buy or rent four fast racehorses, as well as a top driver to win the race for me. But let me tell you, I already have four Arabian stallions to race." He explained his arrangement with al-Hussein. "It is essential that you do not reveal this information to anyone."

Genitos, with a troubled look on his face, started to walk away. But then he turned and stared Emontial straight in the eyes. "What is the name of this sheik?"

"Why do you ask, Genitos? His name is Ostis al-Hussein."

"Well, it's a long story. You never asked me about my life before you bought me as your slave. The only thing you found out was that I could handle a horse. I must tell you now that I was born in Greece to a prominent family. My father was a high-ranking official in the city-state of Salonica. At seventeen, I joined the Grecian people fighting for freedom against the domination of Rome. A Roman general named Octovius captured me, placed me in irons, and sold me as a slave to the senator Romulus."

"Why do you tell me this now, Genitos?"

"Romulus looked me over and had me trained to race his chariot of the white colour. I became his champion driver and was definitely a hero in some people's eyes. I was rewarded with enough money to buy myself out of slavery, but as fate would have it, Romulus' young wife Julia, thirty years his junior, fell deeply in love with me and tried to entice me to be her lover. I refused because I respected Romulus, who had been so good to me. Julia threatened to banish me to the farthest place in the Roman Empire and sell me as a slave. She did that and I was fortunate to be bought by you."

"Can you regain your racing skills?" Excitement mounted in Emontial's voice.

"Those steeds sound like the sort of horses I dream about racing."

"Genitos, we'll travel with haste to Ziz. Eronte, you stay here and build the smoothest fastest, lightest racing chariot. I must take Genitos to meet the sheik formally. When I'm finished, I'll return to Rome to deal with Convictus. We have no time to waste."

"I'll have the chariot ready when you return, Emontial," said Eronte.

"I have been blessed as a Christian by Almighty God and Lord Jesus by having an experienced driver like you, Genitos, appear out of nowhere at such a crucial time. Hallelujah!"

TWENTY-THREE

Surprise Meeting

Arriving at Ziz, Emontial and Genitos went directly to al-Hussein's private tent. Servants ushered them into the sheik's private living quarters. Upon the two visitors entering the palatial room, al-Hussein smiled broadly from ear to ear, jumped up from his couch, and flew over to Genitos, yelling excitedly.

"Genitos, it is you!" al-Hussein said with great happiness. "The greatest driver ever to race in Circus Maximus! You disappeared so tragically! I wanted to know the truth of what happened to you. I always picked you to win, and with your ability, you made me all kinds of money. As a result, the Roman elite treated me with respect, and above all labelled me the intelligentsia of chariot racing." In his exuberance, he grabbed Genitos' hand, pulled him close, and hugged him as if he would a son. "I'm so glad you are alive. The rumour was that you had seduced Romulus' wife and, furious at your disloyalty to him, he banished you to the farthest place from Rome, had you killed, or sold back into slavery."

Emontial, stunned at the scenario unfolding before him, was speechless.

The sheik of Ziz was filled with questions. "What really happened for Romulus to treat you so harshly? Where did you disappear to? Why is it that you're here now?" Genitos opened his mouth, but al-Hussein continued before he could speak. "And Emontial, I'm so pleased to see you. How did you meet this kind man?"

"I'm thrilled that you are excited about Genitos. I originally bought him at the slave market, knowing nothing about his previous life. That's another reason Convictus is furious with me, as he wanted to purchase Genitos for himself. He says I stole Genitos by outbidding him. Genitos became my trusted slave and I promised him freedom if he coached, guided, and protected my adoptive son Eronte as he grew to manhood. Now he's a free man whom I greatly admire, the manager of my factories in Rome."

"Well, now, both of you come immediately," al-Hussein said. "I will be proud to introduce Genitos to my four Arabian stallions. I can't believe it! You, the best driver of all time, will race my treasured stallions. We have so much to reminisce about."

Emontial spoke quickly. "Sheik Ostis, please excuse me. I must urgently return to Rome. Convictus must think I'm on the hunt for horses and a charioteer. I also need to connect with Eronte to see his progress. I will send Eronte to inform you both when all is ready for us to meet in Jerusalem."

"We will await your word," al-Hussein said. "Safe travels, my friend. I will take good care of Genitos. We have much to discuss."

As Emontial left, he could hear the sheik continuing in an excited tone: "You, Genitos, the best charioteer ever, driving my white stallions! No one could beat you at Circus Maximus!"

Genitos spoke humbly. "Well, I didn't win every race, but..."

Their voices trailed off as Emontial passed out of earshot. His heart warmed as he looked back to observe the sheik and Genitos walking arm in arm, heads together in conspiratorial conversation, to the stables where the Arabian stallions were housed.

* * *

Al-Hussein personally introduced each horse to Genitos as though they were human. "Each stallion has a name that suits his personality. Genitos, meet Antar, Asil, Gharib, and Gabbar."[1]

Genitos patted each stallion as he was introduced. "My, you are handsome fellows. You will be a pleasure to drive. Antar, your forehead, eyes, and the flip of your head show your strong determination. Asil, your carriage shows nobility. Gharib, your whole demeanour indicates humility. And Gabbar, what strength! Your hindquarters ripple with muscle!"

---

1 Antar (Strong Warrior), Asil (Noble), Gharib (Humble), and Gabbar (Strong).

He asked the horses if they would follow his directions when he drove them. Each horse pawed the ground and appeared to nod, lowering its head to indicate yes. With a final pat on each muzzle, Genitos told the stallions they would begin training the next day.

The sheik was pleased with Genitos' respectful treatment of his prized stallions.

As the sun rose the next morning, Genitos entered the Arabians' tent and attached the appropriate racing harness to each horse.

"Good morning, gentlemen. Are you ready for training?" With whinnies echoing off the flaps of the tent, Genitos continued. "Antar, I've harnessed you last. With your strength and warrior-like qualities, you are my funalis. Sheik Ostis, do you have a fifth stallion that will keep pace with the other four? That horse will also need a light harness, bridle, and reins."

"Yes, of course, Genitos."

The fifth horse, Hadi, arrived.[2]

"Hadi is a brother and will work alongside the other four racers," al-Hussein said, introducing the stallion to Genitos.

Genitos spoke to each stallion as if the horse was human, explaining that he would lead them through various exercises to win the final race.

Jumping onto Hadi's back, Genitos stood tall. With reins in hand, he led the four Arabian stallions, with full harness and chariot behind, to the sand field that was exactly like the floor of the stadium.

Gently commanding the stallions, Genitos walked them slowly around the field in wide circles, gradually narrowing the circles, and always making left turns. He then trotted them in the same circles. Finally, he galloped them in straight lines, turning left and then racing straight at full speed. Slowing, turning, stopping, slowing, turning, stopping!

The first day, training lasted one hour; the second day, two hours; and the third and fourth days, three hours. Genitos always held the cattail whip in his right hand, snapping it without ever touching any of the stallions. He only stopped training to make an exact outline of the racetrack of the stadium, including the spina and its sharp turns.

---

2 Hadi (The Helper).

On the fifth, sixth, and seventh days, Genitos let the horses rest. He stood by the stallions and spoke softly as he groomed them. He patted each head and lovingly rubbed their withers.

On the eighth, ninth, and tenth days, he raced them on the outlined track while harnessed to a chariot.

"Your wonderful stallions are ready for a practice race today," Genitos reported to al-Hussein. "I am proud to drive and show what this exceptional team has accomplished."

"Let's do the practice race right now, and see the speed and how they turn corners. Come, show me the results of your training."

The stallions performed with strength and stamina. They had mastered the track and the commands of the charioteer.

"I'm amazed at the progress you've made in such a short time," al-Hussein said. "You truly have regained your skill as a champion charioteer."

Genitos did an exceptional job of preparing the stallions, but his joy gave way to melancholy each evening as he sat alone in silence, thinking of Julia, the only woman he had ever loved, but who could never be a part of his life. When questioned by the sheik, Genitos simply said that he was recalling a past relationship. Although al-Hussein knew there was more to be said, he didn't pressure Genitos to reveal his secret thoughts.

TWENTY-FOUR

Racing Chariots

Emontial, upon arriving in Rome, rushed to the chariot factory downtown. Breathless with the excitement of seeing his adoptive son again, Emontial burst through the door.

"Eronte! Where are you? Oh, there you are!" Emontial encircled him in a massive embrace. "Have you had any success in making the chariot lighter?"

"Yes, yes! Come and see!"

After the fond greetings, Eronte showed him the innovative lightweight racing chariot he had designed and built.

"The first chariot is finished, sir. Strong, sixty-centimetre wheels constructed from extremely hard Angleterre wood. Placed over the axle is a small rectangular platform for the charioteer to stand on, surrounded by a low metal railing. The axle hubs are coated with sheep fat to enable the cart to travel faster due to less friction between the axle and the wheels."

"You're amazing, Eronte. A true craftsman! This is a work of art. I'll tell Genitos I commend him for guiding you. Well, all right now, carry on with your work. Again, remember: it's essential that we keep this visit a secret." Emontial, bursting with pride, gave his adopted son one final message: "Pack up this improved chariot and take it to the desert, to the Oasis of Ziz. Genitos is there. He and Sheik Ostis al-Hussein know my plans. Tell them that all is ready. I'll be in contact when you three arrive in Jerusalem. Goodbye, my son. Safe travels."

Feeling pleased and excited at Eronte's hard work, Emontial headed for the stables at Circus Maximus. His purpose was to meet Convictus as if by accident, and convince him that he still needed a driver and good team of horses for their upcoming race.

"Oh! Convictus, hello. I'm surprised to see you! I'm so frustrated. You see, I'm having a terrible time trying to hire a suitable driver and the team I want. Would you consider cancelling our race for Marlan and Paulus?"

Convictus gave him a snarling glance. "Emontial, our bet was a legal document. You either race or forfeit the prize. You got me on legality before. Now it's my turn to get you! There'll be no cancelling this race."

Emontial turned and, stifling a grin, inquired, "Where can I possibly find a racing team and driver in such a short time?"

Convictus smiled sarcastically. "I really wish you good luck, my friend. Ha! Ha!" Laughing uproariously, he drowned out all the other noises of the stables.

"We shall see, my friend," Emontial called back over his shoulder on his way out. "We shall see."

* * *

Meanwhile, Eronte disassembled the chariot, packed it carefully in wooden crates, and travelled to the Oasis of Ziz, guarding the crates all the way. Once he'd arrived safely, al-Hussein, Genitos, and Eronte assembled the prized chariot. Genitos then called the four stallions by name and securely harnessed them.

Genitos drove the stallions at their fastest pace on the field, a simulated stadium racing track. Cheering erupted as the charioteer and his team rounded the last turn and crossed the finish line.

"Wonderful!" al-Hussein cheered. "Wonderful race, Genitos. I cannot believe the speed! Eronte, your chariot design is superb!"

The sheik's whole camp, along with Genitos and Eronte, meticulously prepared to journey to Jerusalem. After five days of preparation, they headed off, arriving at the emporium in the middle of Jerusalem to stable the horses.

Only Emontial knew of the stabling arrangements. To be certain that Convictus' spies wouldn't learn of his involvement, he never visited the stables.

The sheik, Genitos, and Eronte established themselves on the top floor of the inn next door to the stables. This inn had an underground tunnel to the stables which enabled the three to move back and forth, invisible to the outside world.

TWENTY-FIVE

Black Stallions

Convictus, motivated by his innate hatred of Emontial, hired the best racing horses at Circus Maximus. The Roman names for these sleek black stallions were Astutus, Celer, Dominator, and Ferox.[3] This team had won its last twelve races.

These four vibrant Arabian stallions, absolute dream horses, had expressive black eyes, exotic dished heads, beautifully sculpted faces, high necks, and lean, strong legs which made them appear to fly. They had another very important attribute: an almost human competitive disposition demonstrated by their intelligence.

In spite of Marvellus, the charioteer, doubling the outrageous price for the horse team, Convictus paid.

Striding determinedly wherever he went, Convictus yelled at everyone with a cruel and conniving countenance. "I'm going to win! I'm going to win! I know I'm going to win!"

Motivated by revenge for being outbid for Genitos, for the money lost to Emontial at Circus Maximus, and for losing the legal battle for Marlan, Convictus became enraged—so enraged that his efforts to win sparked his insanity.

"I won't have to wait long for my revenge," he said to himself.

---

3 Astutus (Cunning), Celer (Swift), Dominator (Leader), and Ferox (Fierce).

TWENTY-SIX

Race Day in Jerusalem

The next morning, a series of colourful ceremonies began in the centre of Jerusalem. Emontial and Convictus headed the elaborate procession. The two adversaries marched with false admiration, smiling and waving to the laughing crowds who pushed forward to gain a better glimpse of the parade and the two men sponsoring the day. Cheers erupted as they passed.

Emontial waved vigorously. "We're holding an exciting opening, wouldn't you agree, Convictus?"

"Yes, we certainly are. And listen, they're all cheering for us! Little do these crowds know the money we will make from their spending. We will be richer than ever!"

Important civic authorities followed, dressed in impressively coloured robes, some on platforms borne by slaves and others in decorated carriages pulled by horses, elephants, or slaves. Next, the white, red, yellow, and blue chariots paraded by, enhanced by bands playing lively music. White-faced clowns and dancers circulated throughout the marchers, followed by the singing, yelling, and shouting of spectators who crowded in behind.

When the sun was at its highest, the spectacle concluded at the stadium.

The enthusiastic crowd of about thirty thousand entered the stadium. As Emontial and Convictus took their seats, anticipation rustled through the crowd.

Seven silver trumpets blew repeatedly for three minutes. During this time, four white Arabian stallions appeared and stood with majestic posture at the starting line. The charioteer, Genitos, wore a tunic with sleeves called a vestisquadrigaria. He also had a helmet, knee pads, and shin pads, all in bright white.

Four exotic black Arabian stallions appeared directly beside Genitos. They were driven by Marvellus, whose chariot was brilliant red with ivory wheels. He wore the same protective clothing, also in red.

The crowd rose to their feet with a collective roar of appreciation and awe at the spectacle.

Both drivers stared with concentration straight down the spina. Their horses, eager to perform, whinnied and pawed the ground, lifting white dust in the air.

To start the race, trumpets blared, one long and five short blasts, immediately followed by the head dignitaries, Emontial and Convictus, dropping the mappa, a small purple cloth which signalled the charioteers to jump forward.

Both teams bolted ahead. The crowd leaped in the air screaming, yelling, and cheering on their favourite, entranced by the race. People in every corner of the stadium thrust forward to gain the best view.

As slaves removed the first egg from the spina, indicating the completion of the first round, the teams raced side by side. The crowd got noisier and more boisterous as the second and third eggs disappeared. Marvellus tried to get out front, but smashed his chariot wheels dangerously close to Genitos' chariot. The screeching of wheels could be heard above the noise of the stadium.

As the fourth round began, Genitos snapped his whip above the horse's heads and issued a command to his lead stallion: "Gabbar, lead Antar, Asil, and Gharib to stay directly behind Marvellus and his team! Let Marvellus get ahead!"

Convictus, seeing Marvellus in the lead, jumped up and yelled, "I'm going to win! I can feel it! Marlan will be mine."

Genitos held his team until they reached the seventh round. Then, talking loudly to his team, he snapped the whip above their heads and urged them on. "Okay boys, now! Go!"

His white Arabians, nostrils flaring, muscles exploding, and tails held straight, burst forward.

"Gabbar, use your strength. Lead your brothers. On team!"

With an instant change of speed, the white Arabians leaped past the black team just at the finish line and won the race by a nose.

Convictus stared with disbelief. "What? I lost! How could that happen?" He turned on Emontial. "Where did you get those horses? You told me you weren't able to get any. You win this time, but I'll gain my revenge somehow."

The crowd erupted wildly, jumping, dancing, and screaming at the top of their lungs. The head judge ceremoniously descended from the stands to officially crown Genitos the victor. A formal procession led the champions' ceremonial parade to the centre of Jerusalem.

TWENTY-SEVEN

Tearful Parting

The white stallions led the procession, followed jubilantly by Emontial. Convictus cursed as he stomped directly behind Emontial, pushed forward by hundreds of frenzied spectators.

Convictus angrily pulled from his robe a rolled papyrus and thrust it in Emontial's face. "Here! Here are the slavery papers of Paulus. Take them." Turning around, he added under his breath, "I will get revenge. I'll spend all I have to be the victor. Emontial will never embarrass me again."

Genitos and Eronte assisted in trotting the stallions back to the stables. Here, Emontial, elated after his win, met with al-Hussein to pay him for bringing the white stallions and all the necessary equipment for the race.

"Sheik Ostis, I am forever in your debt! Thank you! You have no idea. You just saved my life and made others extremely happy. You did for me what I could never have accomplished. What can I do to thank you? How can I reward you for all you've done for me?"

"Emontial, you gave me extreme pleasure by telling me personally about the sandals of Jesus, which saved your life and started you on a journey to search out Christ's teachings. Your new life in Jesus changed you from a cruel man to a loving and generous person. That's what attracted me to you. Keep on helping others, and I promise you, I will treat everyone in my world in a loving way, as though they were my neighbour." The sheik paused. "You've brought me great pleasure in seeing my children win a challenging race against the best in the Roman world. I thank you for giving me that chance. All I ask is for you to let Genitos drive for me at Circus Maximus when he has spare time from managing your factories."

"Sheik Ostis, I would be honoured to have Genitos drive for you."

The men warmly embraced each other, and then parted. Al-Hussein left Emontial and made preparations to travel to Rome with his whole entourage and race his stallions there.

Emontial hastened to the stable to speak privately with Genitos. Grabbing Genitos by the arm, he led the free man with urgency to a private corner of the stable where spies of Convictus would neither see them nor hear their conversation.

"What do you want, Emontial?" Genitos asked.

"Shh! Genitos, listen carefully! Convictus is in a violent state of hatred against me. He will go to the ends of the earth and spend his entire fortune to destroy me and everything I own. He will cause all my friends and all my businesses to suffer. Beware. Convictus will get his greatest pleasure by hurting you, because he knows my love for you, and your part in guiding Eronte."

"What do you want me to do?"

"He also hates you for your fame, your abilities, your love for Eronte, and your astute business sense. He will tyrannize you by going to Rome's highest court to possess you. As his slave, Convictus would have the power to personally, punishingly, and slowly put you to death.

"Genitos, while you were my slave, I discovered Eronte is the son of a slave woman—a slave woman who Convictus owned. You know Roman law, which states that every child born of a female slave is also a slave. I am fearful that even though Marlan is now in my employ, the Roman court would rule that she was Convictus' slave when I was caring for Eronte. Therefore, if Convictus gains control of all my possessions, he could be able to prove that you are his slave in spite of the fact that I owned you and freed you.

"The sheik of Ziz admires, respects, and loves you. He knows my whole story and is a trusted friend. And, by the way, he wanted me to ask you to drive for him at Circus Maximus.

"For guiding Eronte these many years, I now award you the racing chariot factory in Rome, and the war chariot factory outside the city. Leave immediately in the next hour to escape to Rome. Protect yourself, because Convictus will be plotting harm."

"Thank you, Emontial, for all the opportunities you generously gave me to prove my inner worth. It was a privilege to guide Eronte, and I'm humbled by your confidence in my handling the affairs of your chariot businesses, and especially freeing me from slavery. I am deeply touched. I'll always remember you as the man I most admire. I will leave immediately. Goodbye, my dearest friend."

Genitos hugged Emontial and kissed him on both cheeks. Tears flowed from their eyes, accompanied by sobs of heartfelt emotion.

Genitos left Emontial, located the sheik, and promised he would arrive in Rome shortly. He looked forward to the pleasure of racing the white Arabian stallions at Circus Maximus.

After the tearful goodbye, Emontial with bittersweet emotion, headed out of the stable and climbed into his chariot where Eronte was waiting.

Eronte had a quizzical look as he noticed the glistening in Emontial's eyes. "Are you all right, sir?"

"Yes, better all the time. Drive us home."

Emontial wiped the tears from streaming down his cheeks as he travelled home with Eronte by his side.

I am so fortunate to be with this great, generous man, Eronte thought.

Stopping in front of his house, Emontial looked Eronte in the eyes. "Eronte, I have a joyful surprise for you. I know you'll be very happy, and so will others. I want you to know that I love you with all my heart."

TWENTY-EIGHT

Genitos and Julia

Romulus died two years before Genitos arrived back in Rome with al-Hussein. Having finished a year of mourning, Julia learned that Genitos had returned as a free man and was racing for the sheik. She felt deep in her heart the true, devoted love she still held for him.

What should I do? she asked herself. *I lied to Romulus. I told him Genitos was disloyal to him in trying to seduce me. I can still see the shock on Romulus' face, and the anger he had at my disclosure. Romulus had planned to free Genitos, but my selfish lies banished him to the eastern Mediterranean. I never knew about his whereabouts until now.*

She was rich, powerful, and respected as the widow of Romulus, former head of the Roman senate. She was capable of handling any situation in Rome, except for her love of dear Genitos. She struggled to overcome the dilemma that was tearing her apart. She felt that her world would end before she could see Genitos and ask forgiveness for her selfishness.

Pacing back and forth in her courtyard, she asked herself, *Will Genitos forgive me? How will I approach him to apologize for the horrible lies I told? What can I do to make amends, if they can be made?*

* * *

Genitos once again became the champion driver at Circus Maximus. He walked the streets of Rome with his head erect and thankfulness in his heart.

"Morning, Genitos!" someone called. "Hope you race well today!"

"Thank you. I'll do my best."

When he and Eronte had first come to Rome to manufacture chariots, he walked the back streets to avoid being seen. Now he wondered if Julia would be disturbed to know that he had returned.

Thoughts of Julia flashed constantly through his mind. He knew that Romulus had passed away and that Julia was now free, but she was too far above him in wealth, power, and respect for him to visit. How could he associate with her, having once been her slave?

This quandary tugged at his heart. He thought about every means of seeing Julia.

Where could I arrange to meet her? he asked himself as he walked the street, pumping his fists. *The market? No! Outside the baths? No! On the street? No! Maybe at Circus Maximus? No, no, no!*

All these ideas wound up with the same conclusion: they were impossible to accomplish. Extremely frustrated, Genitos tried to forget about her. The more he worked at ridding his mind of Julia, the more he visualized her and the happiness they could have together.

To calm his mind after a day of racing, he walked along the narrow market streets of central Rome. Recognizing him, people stopped to vigorously shake his hand and pat him on the back. He enjoyed sauntering along Caesar Street outside Circus Maximus, checking the luxurious silks and perfumes and thinking about how Julia would look in the colourful flowing fabrics.

To accommodate the shoppers crowding the market stalls, wagons and carriages were disallowed from travelling those narrow streets from morning until late afternoon. Only necessary vehicles like market carts, public wagons, priestly wagons, and chariots driven in triumphal processions were licensed to travel the narrow streets.

Looking around, Genitos noticed a carruca, a four-wheeled covered carriage. From its ivory, gold, and bronze carvings, it was obviously owned by a senior politician. The driver pulled the two horses up beside Genitos; it hesitated, stopped, and then crawled forward before stopping again.

Genitos was puzzled. Why was this carruca in the street at this time of day? Why was it going so slowly—and stopping? Obviously this politician thought he owned the street.

Inside the carruca, its passenger's heart was torn. What was Julia to do?

Should I speak to Genitos? she wondered. *Does Genitos hate me? What would he do if I called him over and apologized?*

Finally, Julia made her decision. "Driver, pull up beside that tall young man and stop."

She then got Genitos' attention by opening the door halfway. "Genitos, it's me, Julia, in the carruca. Please, come and talk with me."

Genitos recognized her voice and wavered with indecision. Then he bolted to the stopped carriage. Time stood still as they felt their obvious love for each other.

"Genitos, please forgive me," Julia said. "I lied to Romulus. I was very selfish and angry that you wouldn't accept me as your lover. It's because of me that Romulus sent you away. Can you forgive me?"

"Julia, yes, I forgive you. I'm thankful you lied, because that parted us. If I had seen you one more time, I may not have had the courage to resist you, and as a result I would have suffered a tragic death, and you would have suffered shame."

"I love you, Genitos."

"And I will always love you, Julia, but we cannot be together. Being your former slave, I would never be accepted by the people in your life. You would be very unhappy. Please, go, and under no circumstances return to find me. We must not see each other again."

The door shut and the carruca quickly disappeared.

Tears ran down both their faces. They felt warm pleasure from seeing and talking to each other, but agony in their parting. The two lovers each thought, *Is there any way to be together and enjoy our devoted love?*

Emotionally distraught, Genitos kept his head down as he crept to the inn where al-Hussein occupied the entire top floor. Feet leaden, he ascended the stone stairway. When he arrived at the suite, he opened the door and found himself in the midst of a celebration.

"Everyone!" al-Hussein yelled to his guests. "Here is our hero, Genitos, the greatest charioteer in the history of Circus Maximus, who today won the three most difficult races. Come and meet him personally!"

The head magistrate of the Roman court, several senators, and many friends lined up for the privilege of meeting and shaking hands with the celebrity.

Genitos outwardly showed happiness by allowing himself to talk politely to everyone. Once finished, he quickly and quietly left the party.

Al-Hussein, knowing Genitos like a son, rushed to him with a worried expression. He closed the bedroom door. "Son, what's wrong? You left the party without sharing a celebration drink with my guests. They admire you and want to learn the secrets of how you win."

"Please, let me be alone. My heart is broken. There is nothing I can do to heal it."

"What? What happened between the time you raced and when you arrived at the inn?"

"Remember the past love I spoke with you about? Her name is Julia. I hadn't spoken to her in many years. Today, she stopped her carruca beside me on the street, apologized for her lies, and told me she loved me. I told her I loved her, and then sent her away, never to see her again. Her elite society would never accept me."

"Why would they not accept you? You were of the elite in Salonica. And you are the most celebrated charioteer of all time."

"Yes, but I used to be her slave." Genitos paused. "I'm so heartbroken, the willpower that enables me to win eludes me. I could never again race your Arabians the way they need to be raced. I cannot remain here and race for you."

"Lie down and rest, my son. I understand how you feel, having experienced it myself in years gone by. I will search for a solution."

Al-Hussein furrowed his brow and returned to the party. Just as the festivities finished, he asked his friend Legalus, the head magistrate, to remain behind for a minute. He related the entire story of Genitos and Julia in confidence.

"So you see, my friend, I am in desperate need of your advice."

"Yes, Ostis," said Legalus. "Genitos definitely needs help. Let me think deeply on this. There must be a legal solution."

Legalus left, thoughtfully pondering the problem.

When the sheik entered the bedroom to check on Genitos, he found the former slave sound asleep.

Not wishing to disturb his friend, al-Hussein walked pensively to the stables to talk with his horses. As he patted his fine steeds, he discussed in detail all he knew about Julia and Genitos.

"Love is supposed to make people happy, but it's tearing Genitos and Julia apart. This is a terrible situation for two people so deeply in love. What can I possibly do to help them?

None of the ideas he mulled over would provide a permanent solution.

He quickly returned to the inn where he began to arrange a temporary solution. He and Genitos would return to Ziz for a change of venue.

TWENTY-NINE

Happy Meeting

Emontial and Eronte returned home after the races feeling jubilant. The older man buzzed with excitement at the news he would soon share. Arriving at the front of the house, he instructed Eronte to go directly into the sitting room.

"Eronte, I spoke to you earlier of a surprise," Emontial said. "It will be an unbelievable reunion. Go now, enjoy!"

Eronte gave his benefactor a questioning glance as he entered the sitting room. A man and a woman stood before him.

"Eronte, is that you?" the woman said.

Eronte recognized them right away, even though he hadn't seen them in years. "Father, Mother, I can't believe it! Is it really you? What? How?"

His father's arm was around his wife's shoulder, and they both smiled. Without hesitation, they all rushed into each other's arms, joyful tears brimming in their eyes. They embraced with powerful hugs, unwilling to let go. Marlan kept pulling her son close, then stretching him at arm's length to examine him, almost as though she didn't believe he was real.

They kissed, hugged, and cried, letting out soft cries of "I love you," "I've missed you," "Where have you been?" and "What has happened to you over the years?"

Emontial stood in the doorway, acknowledging the happy meeting with a smile. With a wave of his hand, he disappeared into his study, allowing the three to reconnect.

Continuing arm in arm, as if afraid to let go in case this was only a dream, parents and child walked out into the garden and sauntered along. They walked and talked, hoping that time would stop and this festive, joy-filled moment would never end. They stayed together embracing, holding hands, and sharing their experiences after so many years apart, until it was time to retire.

With a heart filled with joy, Eronte quietly entered his benefactor's office, where Emontial sat behind his desk. The younger man was too emotional to speak, but he flung his arms around the older man's neck and hugged him.

"Let go now, son, you're choking me," Emontial said.

Both enjoyed the closeness of the moment, and then parted for the night.

Early the next day, Emontial planned the most festive party he had ever organized. By week's end, the house became transformed. Greenery garlands adorned the portico, wreaths adorned the doorways, and tables were laden with food and decorations. Grapes and other fruit spilled over the bowls. Figs, dates, olives, nuts, bread with olive oil, and platters of roasted vegetables, lamb, and fish were prepared. Cakes in a variety of shapes added a decorative finish to the sumptuous meal. Guests, dignitaries, and government officials arrived in their finest attire.

In the midst of the buzzing conversation, Emontial drew everyone's attention by clanking a cymbal. "Welcome all! I planned these festivities to introduce to you my new manager of all services, Paulus; his wife Marlan, who I have placed in charge of supervising my household; and Eronte, my adopted son, who I have placed in charge of all my business enterprises. To celebrate this occasion, the first thing I instructed Eronte to do is refund each tenant the past year's rent."

The guests roared with approval. The festivities lasted all day and well into the night.

All enjoyed Emontial's warm hospitality. That is, all except one. Convictus, although not officially invited, had come to satisfy his evil curiosity. Previously, he'd only glimpsed Eronte at a distance. He was suspicious of this young man. Upon seeing Eronte, Convictus instantly realized that this was the son of Paulus and Marlan.

I believe I now have positive proof, Convictus thought. *Emontial stole a slave of mine! I will ruin him—and he will become my slave.*

Skulking out of the room, he charged into his chariot. Convictus had the driver gallop the team all the way to his office. Furious to see so much happiness in Emontial, the man he hated, Convictus made a plan to wreak havoc.

He pulled out a bottle of his finest wine. *I detest that man! I will destroy him! I swear, I will spend all my money to retrieve what he has taken from me!*

Convictus drank until he fell to the floor in a stupor.

The next morning, he hired the best legal minds, promising great wealth to the one who could make the four people he named suffer the most. Convictus spent all his conscious time planning ways to devastate Emontial, his former slaves Marlan and Paulus, and especially Eronte, who he perceived to be the cause of all his misfortunes.

THIRTY

Slavery Court

For one full week, joy enveloped Emontial's home. At breakfast on the seventh day, without warning, Roman legionnaires marched into the house straight to the breakfast room, arresting Emontial, Paulus, Marlan, and Eronte.

"What? Stop!" Emontial protested. "What is this? Why are you doing this?"

Unrolling the scroll in his hand, the centurion read, "You, Emontial, are arrested for breaking Roman slavery law. We are transporting you immediately to the official slavery courtroom."

All four were driven out of Emontial's home by the legionnaires, who raised their swords high and shoved their lances forward.

"Chain them if they resist," the centurion demanded.

Disbelief mingled with confusion and fear on the faces of all four prisoners.

The prisoners were roughly deposited in the courtroom from the jail cart and ordered to sit facing Tribune Narcellus.

Convictus, smiling cynically, waited impatiently for Narcellus to ask about the nature of his charge against Emontial. His hate was so strong that it surged from every pore of his being.

Revenge will be sweet, Convictus thought.

Narcellus began, "Convictus, state your criminal charge against Emontial."

"Emontial has broken the most serious Roman slavery law," Convictus began. "This injustice will not only make him my slave, but make me the owner of all he possesses. So what is that offence, you ask? He stole a slave from me! Narcellus, charge Emontial with stealing a slave!" He continued in mocking voice. "Roman law states that if anyone steals a slave, that thief forfeits all his possessions and becomes a personal slave of the person he stole from."

"Yes," Tribune Narcellus commented. "You have stated the law correctly, but be specific as to this charge."

"Eronte is the son of Paulus and Marlan," Convictus said. "Every child of every female slave is automatically a slave."

"Yes, again, that law is correctly stated." Narcellus impatiently tapped his fingers. "Get on with it, Convictus!"

"Marlan was previously my slave, and therefore her son is my slave. Emontial, knowing that Eronte was my slave, secreted him at a school in Rome, thus stealing the child of Marlan from me. Emontial knowingly stole Eronte. Charge him right now, so I can enslave and torture Emontial with hard laborious work."

Scrutinizing the accused, the tribune said, "Emontial, rise and stand before me. I find it hard to believe that you, Emontial, one of the finest men I have ever met, would be subject to this charge. Have you anything to say in your defence?"

"Tribune Narcellus, for the better part of my early life, I was an angry, vicious, cruel, unhappy beast of a man. My hatred was more than double that of Convictus'. As a slum landlord, I never maintained my vast properties. If any tenant complained, I either evicted them with no rent returned or raised their rent. This I did for one reason: to make those tenants suffer worse hardship and poverty. One day, while walking the back streets by my dilapidated properties, relishing in their slum condition with a sarcastic smile on my face, four tenants unexpectedly attacked me. My face, nose, lips, and arms were bloodied; the attackers threw me on the stones in a crumpled heap."

Convictus sneered. "They should have killed you, Emontial!"

"Convictus, there will be no more of that in my courtroom," Narcellus said. "Continue, Emontial."

"My body was bruised and bloodied from top to toe. The attackers left me for dead and I believed the homeless boy, Eronte, saved my life by placing Jesus Christ's sandals on my chest." Emontial choked back tears with the memory of that day. "Eronte later told me that those who attacked and spit on me called me horrible names and felt that they would have been justified if they had killed me. With the help of the boy, I painfully stood up and asked Eronte to help me home.

"Arriving at my place, Eronte explained in a panic that he had to run back to the market quickly so Guandel, the vegetable shop owner, wouldn't beat and starve him for being so slow. I found out later that the owner did beat Eronte and wouldn't give him food, but sent him out with more deliveries. Guandel also threatened him with having to sleep on the street instead of under the vegetable stand on the dirt floor.

"The next day, I sent my slave, Genitos, to find the boy, and bring him to my house to thank the lad. I realized for the first time how precious life is. My new heart, soul, and mind were blessed with thoughts of thanking this boy for helping me. I now desired to be kind to others. The boy was homeless, and had no knowledge if his parents were alive or dead. I placed him in Genitos' care to guide him in all manly ways, and sent Eronte to the finest Roman school.

"Eronte was all alone. As I said, he hadn't heard from his parents for several years. They had disappeared when he was eight years of age. He often wished he knew where his parents were, or if they were still living.

"Jesus performed a miracle that day in gifting me with a new appreciation of life. My attitude changed instantly. I aspired to learn how to follow Jesus' law to use my heart, soul, and mind to treat my neighbour as I would like to be treated. In time, I became a Christian, a follower of Christ."

"Please go on, Emontial," Narcellus said, sensing there was more to the story.

"Prior to Eronte returning home, I came to suspect that Marlan was Eronte's mother. I thought that if I owned her, I could free her from slavery. Then if Eronte was her son, he would be free to peacefully complete his training for the future.

"I obtained Marlan through a bet authorized by this court because I legally bid for and purchased more slaves than Convictus. Marlan, head of Convictus' ladies wear shop, was also rumoured to be the wife of Paulus. Later, I won Paulus through a horse race, and I reunited him with Marlan. Even then I wasn't absolutely certain if these were Eronte's parents, only that they were man and wife.

"Eronte had succeeded at school, becoming a model citizen and a credit to all. I was never certain until all three were reunited that Paulus and Marlan were his real parents. I only suspected it. Now, Convictus wants to gain revenge on me."

Narcellus turned to Convictus. "Did you know this complete story, as told by Emontial?"

"Part of it, but don't ask me to feel sorry," Convictus said. "I will not change my mind. I hate Emontial, and I want him as my slave! The law states that I have the authority. I repeat, as my slave I will work him to death, causing him to suffer slowly. I want my revenge! I want Paulus and Marlan to make me money, and if they don't, I will torture their son with hot irons. Ha! That is my answer, Narcellus. Follow the law. Make your final judgment. Enable me to celebrate my revenge."

"I regret you feel strongly bitter towards Emontial," Tribune Narcellus said. "He reasoned rightfully, except he made one serious mistake against the law. Therefore, against my kind feelings toward Emontial, I am compelled by the law to rule in favour of you, Convictus."

The court sat in stunned silence.

"I knew I'd win! Give me my four slaves!" Convictus jumped up with a scornful smile on his face.

"Emontial, you broke Roman law in trying to do good for Eronte," Narcellus continued. "You should have returned him to Jerusalem to discover definitely if Paulus and Marlan were his parents, especially Marlan his mother. You knew that the law states a child is a slave if the mother is a slave."

"Yes, your honour. I was aware of that fact."

"This is a very difficult decision, because good was intended while an old and established Roman law was broken. Does the good offset the bad? In this case, unfortunately no, because it is a solid, unbreakable law. My final decision is that Convictus will be immediately given Paulus, Marlan, and Eronte as his slaves. Eronte will be a slave, as the Roman law states. However, my ruling for you, Emontial, will be more lenient, because your actions were intended only for good. You will remain free from slavery. My decision is final."

Tribune Narcellus left the courtroom.

Emontial broke into large sobs, his cheeks flooded with tears. Convictus, with a giant snarl, furious with the tribune's decision concerning Emontial, grabbed Eronte roughly by the arm and led him out of the courtroom, followed by Paulus and Marlan, who were in a state of unbelief. They wondered what hardship they would suffer serving this insane, cruel, ignorant master.

THIRTY-ONE

The Magistrate Visits Julia

Upon leaving al-Hussein's celebration party, Legalus contemplated overnight how to help his hero, Genitos.

How can I solve this? Legalus asked himself. *As the second most powerful official in Rome, I should be able to figure out a solution. Let's see now.*

Traditionally, the powerful in society could determine a slave to be free, but even when freed, that slave would never reach the status of the elite. One must be born into it. Therefore, even though a slave was freed, the elite would continue to spurn them like the slave they were.

The problem was, if Julia married Genitos, she would lose her elite status and be ostracized by her former friends. Genitos would also be treated with disrespect and no longer be a hero invited into their homes as an honoured guest. They would both be considered outcasts.

What a situation! I must think of a way to help them. The first thing I need to do is visit Julia. I'll hear the story from her point of view, then decide which steps to take to ensure Julia's happiness.

Over the years, Legalus had wined, dined, and partied with Romulus and Julia. He knew her very well and loved her like a father.

Walking out to his personal chariot, he had the charioteer drive him to the house of Romulus.

Julia sat on the porch with her knees drawn up, head down, and hair askew, devastated over her separation from Genitos. When she heard the chariot halt, she saw the magistrate descend and stride toward the front door. She immediately rushed to greet her old friend and affectionately wrapped her arms around him, clinging to him and shivering with emotion. She kissed him gently on both cheeks and gripped his hand.

"I'm so thankful for your visit," she said as they sat down, facing each other. "Thank you. I need someone to talk to whom I respect and trust. You're here at the right time."

"I am concerned about you, Julia. I love you as I would a daughter. First, is it true that you love Genitos?"

"Yes, I have loved Genitos with all my heart since I first saw him. I knew he loved me, but he would never let me near him when I made feminine advances, because of his utmost respect for Romulus. This infuriated me. Imagine, I, of the highest social elite, unable to entice my own slave. Selfishly, I lied to Romulus, and he banished Genitos to the farthest held Roman territory, to be sold at the slave auction." She proceeded to tell the story of how she'd encountered Genitos on the street—and how he had rejected her. She rocked back and forth with increasing intensity, voice cracking as she broke into wracking sobs. "My life is completely destroyed. I have everything, yet nothing. My heart aches so! Without Genitos, I will not be able to survive. What can I do? What can I do? You are the only one who can help me!"

"Thank you for confiding in me, Julia," Legalus said. "Genitos is a courageous man, and you are a caring, sensitive, intelligent lady. I love you deeply and I honour Genitos. You and he would make a grand couple. At the courthouse, the magistrates will attempt to solve your seemingly impossible problem." He wrapped his arms around her. "We will do our best. Say many prayers to the powers above. I will let you know. Goodbye, my darling Julia."

He leaned over and very gently kissed her on both cheeks. With a quick backward glance, he then left for the courthouse.

Julia, with tears in her eyes, watched wistfully as the chariot disappeared in the distance.

THIRTY-TWO

A Family Enslaved

Convictus charged from the slavery courtroom, cruelly hauling Eronte, with parents Marlan and Paulus following, into a small anteroom beside the portico. It contained only one comfortable leather chair in which Convictus sat, gathering his thoughts, a wicked sneer covering his face.

"Paulus, Marlan, two chariots await outside in which are smartly styled clothing from each of my shops," Convictus said. "Dress yourselves in these clothes. Then follow my instructions exactly. Here are two scrolls, one for each of you. The names of all your former wealthy customers are listed. You are to visit each of them and tell them my shops will reopen in two days. To celebrate, you will be there to personally show elegant clothing only for them." His eyes blazed with determination. "Do exactly as I have demanded. Sell the clothes. Make me money—a great deal of money, or I will personally torture your son. Have I made myself clear? Get out of here! Now! Away from my sight!"

They both left, heads hanging, feet leaden, and desperate with fear knowing that they had to be successful or their son would suffer outrageous punishment.

Grabbing Eronte's arm, Convictus sneered through bared teeth, "You are now my slave, but since you've never been a slave, I intend to have you taught what it really means."

Eronte stiffened but continued to stand erect. Knowing that he had to take this abuse, he decided not to rebel. Inwardly he questioned, *What is he going to say and do next?*

"The cruellest slave encampment will teach you the hard way," Convictus continued in a strident tone. "Imprisoned directly beneath your feet are the worst, cruellest slaves in the Roman Empire. They're all killers, thieves, or mentally unfit. Realizing your elite background, they will show you no mercy. You will beg for food. Follow their orders, or they'll beat you. They may even beat you if you do follow orders. Ha!"

Eronte forced himself to stand tall, even as his confidence wavered.

"I shall leave you imprisoned there for a year," his master said. "When I return, I will see if you've survived. You, an educated man in slavery, tortured by the worst slaves in the Empire. Guards, grab Eronte, chain him, and drag him to his prison!"

Convictus' ruffians, one on each side, roughly hauled Eronte in chains to the musty cell. Convictus then had the chains removed and Eronte thrown in among the eighty slaves, each of them burly and ragged. With a sneering smile, Convictus slammed shut the iron gate.

He called upon the self-appointed head of these so-called city slaves, a beastly man of three hundred pounds. He was six feet, seven inches, with rippling muscles due to his twelve years rowing Roman galleys.

"Criminus, this new slave is a spoiled rich person," Convictus said. "Train him to be the most degraded slave in the Empire. I promise, if you succeed in your cruelty by torturing and humiliating him, I will make you a free man."

Pleased with his plans, Convictus rushed back to his office.

* * *

Criminus tyrannically ordered the other slaves to work, but he did not work himself. City slaves kept the streets clean through driving the honey wagon, picking up garbage, gathering dead bodies left on the streets, and sweeping, or washing the streets of excrement and vomit. These slaves were the most incorrigible slaves, older slaves, or slaves who needed to be taught a lesson about how to be grateful to lead the life of an ordinary slave.

Criminus, taking his new appointment seriously, glared at this new slave and threw his neck cloth in the darkest corner of the cell. "Pick up my neck cloth with your teeth," he said. "Crawl on your knees and hands with my cloth in your mouth, and bring it to me like a dog."

The other inmates shrank to the opposite corner, huddling together in fear.

Eronte hesitated, then stood still, straight, and tall with a determined and scrutinizing stare at Criminus.

"Do as I tell you or I'll personally punish you in a very painful way," Criminus said. "Isn't that right, men?"

All the other slaves shuddered. One man, Thomonus, yelled, "Young man, do as Criminus tells you or you'll be maimed for life. He'll break every bone in your body."

Eronte stood firm, continuing to silently stare into Criminus' eyes. Criminus, rippling and flexing to show off his muscles, lunged towards Eronte. Seeing the enemy advance, Eronte backed up and checked himself into a defensive position.

Eronte had studied fighting for several years at the Romulus academy, and under Genitos' teaching he had become the champion of champions. No one had ever come close to beating him. Criminus was in for a surprise.

Criminus charged full speed, swinging his left fist at the younger man's jaw.

Staring directly into the man's commanding eyes, Eronte grabbed the gigantic man's wrist with his right hand, jumped to the left and stuck out a leg, moving his right hip quickly against his enemy's bulk. He let Criminus fly through the air on his own inertia, crashing into the stone wall, stunning himself. Eronte kicked him brutally between the legs. Placing his full weight with his knee on Criminus' chest, Eronte grabbed the criminal's hair, pulling it hard to crunch his head against the floor while he punched Criminus several times, knocking the giant unconscious.

Eronte stood, walked calmly to pick up the cloth he'd been ordered to hold in his mouth dog-like, and returned with it to the crumpled, bloodied heap of humanity on the floor. He kicked the man over and tied Criminus' hands behind his back with the cloth. He then rolled him face up again.

Standing over Criminus, Eronte addressed the other slaves who had emerged from their corner of safety in a state of relief and disbelief. "Men, your terror is over. This tyrant will never hurt anyone again. I'll see to that.

We'll give him only enough water to keep him alive. We'll feed him no food. Those of you who were tortured by him, please come and stand by me."

For several minutes, no one moved. The silence was deafening while the men considered Eronte's request. Then, hesitantly, twenty men stepped forward, and Eronte numbered them.

"Number five, what torture did he inflict on you?" Eronte asked.

"He broke the fingers on my left hand because I didn't comb his hair properly."

"Do not be afraid, for he will never touch you again."

Picking up a battered bowl, Eronte filled it with water from the urine puddle on the dirty floor. He threw the water in Criminus' face and waited for him to awake.

There was complete silence in the room as Criminus screamed piercingly. "Mercy! Have mercy on me!"

"You, Criminus, are no longer the tyrant in this cell. We are all equal; even you will be allowed to be one of us if you behave as you are told. If you don't do as we say, I'll punish you and make you suffer worse than you have made these men suffer."

Criminus continued pleading for mercy.

"How much mercy did you give these men when they pleaded for your mercy? Numbers one to four, step forward and stand around this man who tortured you. Each of you has the choice of hitting him anywhere, kicking him anywhere, or forgiving him and doing nothing."

All four stood and stared coldly at Criminus.

"No! No!" the man cried. "Please, don't hit me or kick me. I'm sorry for what I have done to each of you. I will never do it again. I plead with you to forgive me for the terrifying pain I inflicted on you. I beg you not to torture me anymore."

The four men swung their fists menacingly, kicking their feet in the air towards him.

Eronte spoke in a quiet voice. "Kick or hit him if you want to punish him. This will be your only chance for revenge."

Numbers one to four stood tall, stared at each other, and nodded in silent agreement. They lowered their fists and feet and retreated to join their fellow slaves.

With a warm smile, Eronte addressed each man. "Grace given by you will help this man be a better person. You have acted in the proper manner, following my Jesus' teachings by treating another as you would like to be treated."

The other sixteen prisoners who had been brutalized by Criminus acted in the same manner, giving him grace.

Each day, Criminus begged for mercy. When five days had passed with no food and very little water, they untied him and sat him up against the cold stone wall.

Once Criminus was untied, Eronte spoke up. "All of us are equal. From now on we'll all share the work, especially the loathsome jobs like the honey wagon, picking up dead bodies, and cleaning up excrement. Each of us will help our fellow slaves, treating each other like we ourselves would like to be treated. All food will be divided equally. Our sleeping places will be made as comfortable as possible. We'll take turns resting in the best spots. We'll all smile as we work. No one will complain.

"The jailors will note the change not only in our attitudes, but in the better work habits we practice. We'll keep ourselves clean, and our uniforms as respectable as possible. Listen carefully. When our new practices are noticed, we'll possibly be given better food and clothing, and others will think positively of us. Believe it or not, some slaves hearing of our new circumstances might want to join us in being city slaves." The other slaves looked at each other with nods of approval. "Remember this most crucial message: treat your fellow slaves as you would like to be treated."

All the slaves smiled, even Criminus. They agreed that Eronte was right in everything he had proposed. All stood, clapped, and cheered Eronte. There was a new feeling of willingness and camaraderie within the cell as all prepared to do the best they could in spite of their impoverished existence.

THIRTY-THREE

The Magistrate's Plan

Legalus called a private meeting with his colleagues to find a solution to the difficult situation of how to reunite Genitos and Julia.

"Gentlemen, as you know, tradition dictates that one must be born into the elite class or be invited and accepted on merit. You all know Genitos and my old friend Romulus' widow, Julia. Genitos and Julia are deeply in love but cannot be together. Genitos, in spite of his hero charioteer status, would never be accepted by the socially elite because he was Julia's slave. We cannot create a law to force the highborn to welcome outsiders. I lay awake all last night thinking of an answer to help my dear Julia, but have not succeeded. Can any of you suggest a solution?"

After some discussion, followed by reflective thought, the deputy magistrate spoke up. "Was not Genitos a Greek officer, fighting for Salonica's freedom from Roman control? If memory serves me well, his father was a political official. Therefore, Genitos was born a member of the elite social strata in Greece."

"Yes, I do believe you're right," Legalus said. "Wait a minute! I have an idea! What if we arrested Genitos as an escaped political prisoner and sent him back to Greece? He would then regain his elite status in his home country, thus becoming equal in class to Julia, and he could return to Rome and be with her."

With handshakes, and salutes all round, the magistrates raised arms in the air signifying their consensus in favour of the arrest. All agreed that their decision must be kept in strictest confidence.

The question was, how could they have Genitos publically arrested in a way to make the elite curious as to what had happened? The magistrates came up with several ideas. The one they agreed on would produce the most shocking rumours to arouse curiosity. It would be an unheard of spectacle, one that only the magistrates could make happen.

But first, Genitos had to be convinced to race again at Circus Maximus.

Arriving at al-Hussein's inn, Legalus found Genitos in the garden and took him aside.

"I have a way to enable you and Julia to be together," Legalus said. "You must give me your full trust. First, you must regain your mental strength to win one more race against Marvellus. My subsequent plan will enable you to be equal to the Roman elite. If you follow my instructions, and all goes well, you will be happily married to Julia."

Genitos' shoulders slumped. "I want to race again, but I'm so destroyed mentally. My racing days are over. I lack the courage to face the difficult challenges needed to win races."

"I ask that you race only three races on one day, the first two for practice, to regain confidence. Then in the seventh, the final and most celebrated race, win against Marvellus. I'm certain that when I speak with Sheik Ostis he will be proud to have you race his white Arabian stallions once again to victory."

Genitos' voice quivered with emotion. "Thank you for your supreme effort to help me. I will try to do as you ask, but I'm not certain I can fulfill your wishes. All I know is that I love Julia. Give me at least three weeks to prepare myself."

"I'll tell you more as soon as I have it arranged. Trust me. Tell no one, not even Emontial or Julia, of our discussion. Goodbye."

Genitos replied tentatively, shaking inside from mental fatigue. "Yes, yes, I'll do as you ask."

After a night of tossing, turning, and vivid dreams of Julia, Genitos awoke before sunrise with a renewed resolve to visit the country farm where retired racehorses were treated like royalty. They were allowed to roam freely in grassy pastures, bedded in individual stalls, and given rations of grain from neighbouring fields. In the past, Genitos had frequently travelled there to gain solace as he groomed the great horses and shared his secrets with them. They were his almost-human friends. When he appeared, they would whinny gently, trotting to him as he spoke and patted each one.

For a month, he sheltered at the farm without any visitors, renewing his confidence. He raced some of his favourite horses in the fields. He worked the horses hard physically, and at the same time gained physical stamina for himself.

He then returned to the sheik's lodging at the inn.

"Genitos, you look good," al-Hussein said. "How go the preparations?"

Genitos answered with renewed strength. "Sheik Ostis, I am ready."

"Excellent!" The sheik placed his hands on the younger man's shoulders. "I am proud of you for your hard work. I know you will succeed."

"Thank you for understanding."

"I will notify the head magistrate that you've gained the confidence to race once again."

THIRTY-FOUR

Race Day in Rome

Legalus scheduled this particular race, the largest of the year, to coincide with the Emperor's birthday. The Emperor himself would sit high in his private box, styled in royal purple. Circus Maximus would be filled to capacity with people waiting in long lines to get even a small glimpse of the Emperor.

A rumour passed quickly from mouth to mouth that the seventh and most important race would include teams driven by Genitos and Marvellus, the two winningest charioteers to ever race at Circus Maximus. Everyone belonging to elite Roman society would attend in all their finery. The whole city was abuzz with anticipation.

Knowing the importance of this day, Legalus organized the races to enable Genitos to practice in the first and fourth races to raise his spirits, and be ready for the seventh race to defeat Marvellus.

The morning commenced with the charioteers driving ornately decorated chariots pulled by beautifully groomed Arabian horses, followed next by acrobatic clowns. Important people like senators were carried in padded chairs. Finally, the Emperor himself, carried by slaves and circled by his entourage, waved and smiled as he passed through the streets lined by cheering people. Thousands walked, danced, or ran while parading in the procession. The singing and cheering echoed off cobblestones as the throng passed.

All the participants finally entered the portico at Circus Maximus. The noise of laughter, yelling, and cheering was so deafening that citizens were unable to hear ordinary conversation. Happiness exploded everywhere.

THIRTY-FIVE

New Leader

During the year Eronte was in prison, Convictus imagined Eronte as a dirty, demoralized, starved, terrorized slave. In reality, Eronte emerged as a respected leader, encouraging all city slaves to strive and be proud of the streets they cleaned. City officials couldn't believe what was happening. Criminus, smiling continuously, was no longer the cruel tyrant but a changed man who helped alongside the other slaves; he even worked longer hours than the rest of them. The officials noticed that the slaves kept themselves and their uniforms as clean and neat as possible. They appeared content working longer hours than before, and they didn't complain.

Through negotiations with Eronte and Criminus, the officials provided healthier food, better uniforms, and cleaner living conditions. Everyone was satisfied.

These slaves completed their tasks in a professional manner, and thus the city's expenses decreased. They received the best physical treatment of all slaves. As Eronte had predicted, certain other slaves asked their masters to place them with the city slaves. In fact, there was a waiting list in order to be picked to be a city slave.

Eronte, knowing that Convictus would soon arrive to claim him for his personal slave, called the men together and praised them for their accomplishments. They all, in turn, thanked Eronte for teaching them Jesus' way of living: to show their love of others by treating everyone as they would like to be treated.

"Fellow slaves, tomorrow I will not be here," Eronte said on his last day. "I know not where I will be or what I will be doing. Convictus will be here in the morning to collect me."

Boos, hisses, and loud, panic-stricken voices resounded off the stone walls of the cell.

Eronte continued in measured tones. "Remember always that you are all equal. Keep smiling. Continue working in that way, and you will be successful. Since I'm leaving, you need to appoint a leader equal to each of you, to ensure that all forthcoming jobs will be handled effectively, properly, and without prejudice. So now, I have a very important question to ask. Your decision will affect each one of you. Remember, this is a very important decision. Who do you wish to replace me as your leader?"

Thomonus raised his hand high. "I want Criminus!" All slaves stood, stomping feet, clapping hands, and cheering to show their enthusiasm. "Criminus, we all agree. Will you lead us, being our equal?"

Criminus stood and humbly stammered, "Fellow slaves, I–I–I d–don't understand why you are appointing me, the one who tortured, beat, and humiliated you. I do not deserve this honour. You should appoint someone who has always done right, even when he suffered my torture."

Thomonus jumped up and spoke loudly. "You, Criminus, are the one we want. You changed completely over this past year and have become the most beloved slave amongst us. Almighty God, through His Son Jesus, has given you His grace. You have been forgiven. You are a different person, a new man, a man of understanding. With your tender kindness, you inspire us all to be kinder human beings. Remember, as Eronte said, we are all equal. If you need help, say so, and we will do our best to help you."

Tears clouded Criminus' black shiny eyes. He humbly searched the faces. "Fellow slaves, I have come to love you all. Thank you for this honour! I accept! I will work hard to fulfill this position."

Eronte thanked all for their heartfelt decision and then walked over to Criminus. "Well, big guy, you've made the right choice to lead a Jesus-filled life, and you've gradually learned to treat your fellow slaves as you would like to be treated. Some people start out with good intentions but fall back into their own old ways. I know that with Jesus' help you will succeed to lead these men in the right direction. Congratulations."

Criminus' loud voice cracked with emotion as his burly arm circled the younger man. "Eronte, thank you for teaching us to show our love to Jesus. We are going to miss you and your kind wisdom. May God keep you safe."

Eronte stood tall and proud, outwardly showing his respect for the other slaves, yet inside he hid his trepidation of the treatment he would receive from the beast Convictus.

All his fellow slaves wished Eronte well. Then they went back to work, happy in their decision to elect Criminus as leader.

THIRTY-SIX

Convictus Claims Eronte

Early the next morning, Convictus arrived to collect his slave. He expected to see Eronte gaunt, dirty, bruised, and completely humiliated. Although it was commonly known that there was a change in the working condition of the city slaves, Convictus, with his self-consumed nature, was oblivious to it; he was only interested in his riches and evil plans.

He strode into the slavery building, a cynical sneer on his face, and descended the stairs to the city slave quarters.

Arriving at the jail cell, he yelled, "Eronte, get out here! Let me see how dismal you are! You better have learned how to behave! I'll give you the honour now of being my personal slave. Ha!"

Eronte did not appear.

Convictus stomping furiously. "Eronte, get out here immediately!"

Criminus suddenly appeared, as though out of nowhere, and turned to Convictus with cold eyes.

"Where is Eronte?" Convictus asked. "Bring me my slave. If you tortured and taught him manners as I instructed, I'll set you free as promised."

"No!" Criminus roared. "Listen to me. Eronte is the most intelligent, courageous, and hardworking city slave. He taught us to realize that helping others, treating them like we would want to be treated, brings real joy. We can smile, be proud, and do our best in whatever circumstances life imposes. You are very fortunate to have Eronte as your slave. You should free him. Allow him to teach you how to be satisfied with your fortune, and not be the bitter, unhappy beast you are.

"Face it, you have no friends, only jealous, conniving enemies. Your power and riches do not bring you joy. You pretend to be happy with your cynical smile, but you don't fool anyone. I repeat: free Eronte, let him teach you, and you'll become happy and, more importantly, respected for your ability to treat others like you would like to be treated.

"I was richer than you, but I lost everything due to a similar attitude to yours. I became a galley slave for a decade, and for a time I was the unhappiest, most merciless slave in the world. No more. I will return with the wisest man I have ever known."

Criminus turned to leave.

Convictus thought to himself, *When I return from the highest courts as the richest man in the Roman Empire, I will buy Criminus, personally torture him, and cut off his ugly head to be mounted as a trophy.*

Eronte strode toward to Convictus, clean and neatly dressed.

"What? How?" Convictus said. "You're supposed to be beaten black and blue, dirty, bloody, with torn clothes falling off you. Criminus, hear me. You didn't follow my directions, and you will never be free!" He stared glazingly at Criminus. "I will personally teach Eronte the despair of being my slave. Guards, chain his arms and legs and deliver him to my office immediately."

After hauling Eronte roughly through the streets, they deposited him in Convictus' office. He stood as upright as possible in chains at the front of Convictus' imposing wooden desk.

With a calm and strong demeanour, Eronte waited an hour for Convictus to finally arrive.

"Take his chains off!" Convictus said when he arrived. He sat smugly on the corner of his desk. "You have the honour of being my personal slave. I'm traveling straightaway to Rome, to the highest court in the land. My burning desire is to enslave Emontial, own everything he has accumulated, and be the richest man in the Roman Empire. I hope you realize that you, and only you, have made it possible to destroy your so-called benefactor." He gave a mocking bow, his voice dripping with sarcasm. "I thank you very much! Pack my trunks and carry them to the waiting chariot. Then stand at attention until I get there. You will walk, or run, following the chariot wherever and however far. If you get too far behind, I'll have you whipped like a horse, or a dog. Ha! Go!"

Eronte was never whipped. With great strength, determination, and spirit, he stayed close behind the chariot in spite of all the miles to the seaport. There, he loaded the heavy trunks and climbed aboard to be stuffed in the hold with the trunks for the entire voyage, thrown only leftovers to satisfy his hunger.

Convictus' galley crossed the Mediterranean to Rome where Eronte unloaded the baggage and trudged behind the chariot to the inn near the courthouse. Little did Eronte know that the physical stamina and strength he'd gained from all this running and lifting would one day impact many.

THIRTY-SEVEN

Courts and Races

Convictus had planned his court appearances in detail. The legal process to enslave Emontial would take five morning court appearances over a period of five days.

On the first day, the facts of the case were analyzed. On the second day, every Roman law pertaining to the case would be studied. On the third day, the facts and laws would be scrutinized, to judge whether the case was worthy of continuing. On the fourth day, all magistrates would make their decision privately, and present their opinions to the head magistrate, Legalus, who would make the final ruling. On the fifth day, the court would reconvene with all parties and Legalus would read the final verdict.

After the second morning, Convictus hauled Eronte with him to sit in his private box at Circus Maximus, directly beside the Emperor's box. Convictus bet thousands more than ever on Marvellus and his black Arabian stallions in the seventh race, even though Marvellus had previously lost to Genitos with this same team of horses.

Convictus grabbed Eronte by the arm and shoved him into the farthest corner of his box, out of earshot from the head magistrate.

"You, rush down to the stables," Convictus demanded. "Search out Genitos! Demand that he come second in the seventh race, letting Marvellus win. Tell him that if he doesn't comply, I will starve and beat you almost to death. Go, now!"

Eronte hurried obediently. *Convictus is fixing the seventh race,* he thought. Roman law punished anyone who fixed a race with a year in solitary confinement and daily torture, followed by beheading. If Convictus was convicted of fixing a race, Eronte knew he and Genitos would be considered accomplices and suffer the same consequences. *What should I do?*

Before arriving at the stables, Eronte decided to suffer rather than hurt Genitos, his most trusted friend.

Eronte's heart warmed at the sight of the charioteer, patting and talking to his white stallions. Both men screamed with delight, grabbed each other in a crushing hug, and celebrated as true friends. They told each other the happenings in their lives.

"Why did Convictus allow you to come see me?" Genitos asked. "You are his personal slave, and he hates me. Wait a minute! Don't tell me. As the champion driver, I hear rumours. My informants tell me that Convictus bet three million denarii on Marvellus in the seventh race. Did he send you to somehow convince me to let Marvellus win?" Before Eronte could confirm the rumour, Genitos gave him a word of caution. "Don't utter a word. If you do, you could be guilty of helping to fix a race, and we would both lose our heads. Stay with me until the seventh race is about to start, and then return to the stands. If what I'm thinking is true, I'll have a great deal of fun torturing Convictus."

* * *

At the stadium boxes, Convictus noticed that Legalus shared the Emperor's box, though he was seated at a lower level.

Legalus turned towards Convictus. "I'm proud to be the chief official today," Legalus said, "which means I have the honour of dropping the mappa for the first six races. The Emperor himself will drop the mappa for the seventh and most prestigious race. I'll also receive all monies lost by the bettors after the winners are paid. I tell you this because I know you bet three million denarii on Marvellus and the black stallions. I also know that you sent Eronte to the stables to talk with Genitos. Having been in charge of racing for several decades, I'm knowledgeable that some men, no matter how rich they are, conspire to make money the easy way. The easy way is to fix a race so a certain team comes first. I'm not accusing you of this offense, but if I found out that you cheated, I would have you thrown into solitary confinement for one year and then beheaded."

Convictus squirmed, sweating profusely, unable to speak.

"I would take great pleasure sentencing you to this punishment because of your extreme cruelty to others. You treat everyone, especially Eronte, in horrific ways. You think you're the centre of everything. You want me to hurt Emontial, the kindest man I know, who would even help you if you were in trouble."

Convictus fell backwards into his seat and turned ashen white. He shook violently. There was no way to stop the race being fixed. It was too late. The seventh race was about to begin. His fate was sealed.

"Excuse me," Legalus said. "I must now stand at the front of the box and prepare the mappa for the Emperor to drop. I hope I'm wrong about your involvement in the race."

Convictus grabbed a bottle of pure spirits and swallowed the contents. Tears came in torrents as he realized that if Marvellus won, he would suffer as the magistrate had predicted. He saw in detail the degree to which his selfishness and greed were destroying him, and causing him to lose all he had acquired over the years.

What a catastrophe! It would be his ruination to lose everything in an instant.

At that moment, in his horror, Convictus had a glimpse of what he should do to lead a better life.

THIRTY-EIGHT

Emperor's Seventh Race

Legalus dropped the mappa six times. In those races, Marvellus won races two and five by a wide margin. Genitos came fourth in the first race and third in the fourth race. The wise magistrate purposely put Genitos in different races than Marvellus so that the only race in which Genitos and Marvellus would face each other was the seventh.

The crowd pressed forward as the seventh and final race was announced. By lot, Marvellus drew the first starting gate and Genitos drew the fourth.

The Emperor stood waving to the crowd of spectators as thunderous trumpets announced the colourful ceremony announcing the seventh race in honour of the Emperor. The stands reverberated as everyone yelled, "Emperor Caligula, happy birthday, happy birthday, happy, happy birthday!"

Caligula waved his arms wildly up and down to show his thanks to the excited crowd. Then he picked up a huge multi-coloured mappa handed to him by the head magistrate. Placing his arm high above his head, he signalled the charioteers to move quickly to their starting positions.

At the Emperor's signal, the seven charioteers bolted forward. Each team battled to gain the first position. Marvellus jumped out to a lead of three lengths ahead of the six other chariots. Genitos intentionally started out last to torture Convictus. But with Marvellus so far in the lead, Genitos had work to do.

Jostling to overtake Marvellus, two chariots clanked their wheels and the carts flipped over. One driver was thrown into the air and landed in a heap, while the other was dragged by the runaway team into the spina. Genitos was able to guide his team around the carnage and continue to pursue his rival. The second and third laps were completed without incident.

Marvellus whipped his team to stay in the lead. After the third egg was removed, in the fourth lap, another crash brought the crowd to their feet. They jumped, screaming with excitement when another charioteer missed the turn and crashed into the end of the spina, killing himself. Genitos swerved, his cart rocking but staying upright, and he was able to circle around, reaching the third position. There were now four teams left in the race.

In the fifth lap, Genitos was still third but he had eased a bit closer to second place.

When the sixth egg was removed, Genitos was in second. Glancing behind, Marvellus saw his rival approaching.

"Run! Run!" Marvellous cried, furiously whipping his stallions.

Speaking to his Arabian treasures, Genitos flicked his whip and snapped it above their heads, urging them on. "Antar, now! Asil, Gabbar, Gharib, forward! Go! Fly! Hurry! Bring us home!"

One hundred yards narrowed to twenty yards. Then there were only ten yards to the finish line.

The teams pushed forward, using their greatest strength, racing neck to neck. At the finish line, Genitos' team won by a nose, passing Marvellus and his black Arabians. Genitos had made the impossible become possible.

The crowd went wild, jumping up and down and yelling, "Genitos! The greatest racer ever has won the most challenging race!"

Convictus collapsed into his seat. Returning to the box, Eronte helped him to his feet.

Convictus, free from the fear of punishment, learned nothing from these horrible happenings. He immediately scorned the money loss, staring at Legalus, but not daring to say anything as his own court judgment was forthcoming.

In spite of his minutes of self-torture, Convictus still focused on Emontial. Under his breath, he uttered, "I will ruin him and make him my slave!"

Convictus maintained his dictatorial way of handling matters. Focusing on revenge, he coveted Emontial more than ever and desired to own everything the man possessed. Convictus' fervent fantasy was to be the richest man in the Roman Empire, no matter what he had to do to accomplish it.

As was the custom for the winner of the most celebrated race, Genitos drove slowly around the track, bowing his arms and waving to the cheering crowd. When he arrived in front of the imperial box, he was surrounded by the elite of Rome and the exuberant crowd. Genitos bowed and saluted the Emperor.

The crowd gasped as an unexpected event occurred. One hundred legionnaires poured onto the racetrack and surrounded Genitos. They grabbed him roughly and chained him. To the crowd, this seemed very cruel and painful. At the same time, a large cart with a jail cell rolled up and the legionnaires hauled him inside. The cart left the stadium quickly to avoid the enraged crowd.

THIRTY-NINE

The Ship Sails

The fast-moving cart lost the crowd by heading for a galley tethered to the dock in the harbour. Arriving at the galley, Genitos was released from his cell and tossed roughly aboard. He fell into the hold.

Once inside, out of sight, the captain gently set Genitos free from the chains.

"Welcome aboard, sir," the captain greeted him warmly. "My galley is at your command."

"What? Why? I don't understand."

Bowing deeply, the captain continued with a conspiratorial chuckle. "The head magistrate, my friend, ordered me in secret to have your arrest look authentic. In reality, this was part of the plan for you to escape. Legalus has instructed me to serve all your needs."

Genitos was still in shock. "I'm so grateful. Legalus certainly planned a very strange escape. Now I understand his plan and why he told me to trust him totally."

"Quickly, untie the ropes and pull up the anchor!" the captain ordered his sailors. "I hear the angry noise of the crowd!" He turned to Genitos. "We must sail immediately to get away from those who want to free you. They think you've been punished for being an escaped political prisoner."

"We are ready to depart now, sir," hollered the first mate.

"Cast off, men! Genitos, Legalus said you would instruct me as to the destination. What port do I sail to?"

"Take me to Salonica, my home city. My parents live there, if they are still alive."

"Yes, sir." The captain stood at attention and saluted Genitos, then turned and yelled at the top of his commanding voice: "Row out of the harbour and set sail for Salonica." He turned back to Genitos. "Sir, if the weather is fair, we will arrive four days hence. If you need anything, my men have orders to do as you command. Legalus honours you. I, my men, and this boat are yours for as long as you need. My orders are to stay with you to help you achieve your goals. I repeat, we will do whatever you ask of us."

"Thank you! Well then, Captain, make this galley sail and row as fast as it can to Salonica."

"Yes, sir! Are you in need of anything now, sir?"

"Only peaceful quiet, the sun, and the sea air filling my heart."

The galley lunged forward as the ship's booming drum was beat at a certain rhythm to order the slaves to row in an orderly manner.

Genitos remained in the hold until they were out of sight of the gathering crowds, but then he sat on the sun-filled deck, his hands cupping his knees. Legalus' plan had surprised him, but so far it was working.

The Roman elite will be curious as to why I was arrested, he mused. *They will learn in time that I come from the Grecian elite.*

He had so many questions. Were his parents alive? Was his father still in government? How could he prove to the Roman elite that he was equal? Would Julia accept his love for her?

Julia, my dearest Julia, my hope is to be together soon.

Upon docking four days later in Salonica harbour, Genitos remarked, "Captain, you have fulfilled your duty in giving me safe passage. Tie the galley here and wait for my further instructions. I don't know how long I will be. I'll keep you informed."

Watching the young man disembark, the captain gave a final salute.

FORTY

Salonica

Genitos disembarked and headed for his father's home. Rushing into the courtyard of the lavish home, he spotted his mother sitting in the garden. She glanced up to see her son approaching and squealed with joy. Coming out on the porch to see what was making the commotion, his father broke into a wide smile. Genitos greeted and hugged his parents. His eyes watered and his voice cracked with emotion.

"Father! Mother! Let me look at you both. You haven't changed! How wonderful to see you again. I have so much to tell you!"

Tears came in an avalanche to Pedaeus and Anthela. They held each other and their son closely, never wanting to let go.

"Genitos, is it really you, son?" his mother Anthela asked.

"Son, you're home, after all these years!" said Pedaeus. "We thought you had died in the fight for freedom and were certain you were lost forever. Our grief continued through all the years. Unbelievable! Now you're standing here whole and well! Come, sit on the porch so we can hear all about what has happened to you."

"I thought of you both every day," Genitos said. "Not one day were you absent from my mind. I love you both. I've missed you. I've had quite a life, from being a slave to managing a chariot factory and driving as a famous charioteer at Circus Maximus." He paused. "But more of that later. I desperately need your help, for I love a Roman woman, Julia, with all my heart. Although she loves me, I am unable to be with her because for a time I was her slave and the Roman elite would never accept me, and it would ruin her life. To be happy, I must be with Julia as my wife. Father, I need your help to somehow overcome this problem. Do you know of any way I could lose my slave status to join Julia as part of high society in Rome?"

Genitos' parents were happy beyond belief that he was alive. Although they had been apart for many years, he believed that his parents, with the closeness they shared, could get at the root of the problem and realize Genitos' agonizing situation. Concerned for the future, they stared at their son, wondering what could be done to help him.

Early the next morning, Pedaeus walked to Salonica's government building with a spring in his step. He was chairman of the city-state assembly, which was comprised of twenty-four elected representatives.

When the assembly met that day, Pedaeus opened the meeting with one purpose in mind. "Representatives, we gather this morning to vote on the motion of whether to appoint a politically qualified man to represent us in Rome. Our debate is over, having lasted several days. It is now time to vote yea or nay when I ask you to voice your decision. What is your choice?"

The assembly roared with the noise of all present: "Yea!"

"The yeas are unanimous. We will now seek men who wish to hold that position. Each one will come before us. We will start the hearings seven days from tomorrow. This assembly is ended."

Pedaeus rushed home where he and Anthela met with Genitos on the porch.

"Genitos, your mother and I think we have found a way for you to return to Rome as a member of the Grecian elite," Pedaeus said.

"Thank you, Father, but how?"

"Well, our assembly requires a qualified man to be our ambassador to Rome. He must be a member of the Grecian elite, well educated, have vast life experiences, and have fought for the freedom of Salonica. Seven days from today, my assembly will hear and question men who apply for this position. Three men have already shown interest. Here is your chance to return to Rome on Julia's level, maybe even higher. The Roman elite will be pleased to have you as an acquaintance, yet alone a friend. You are ideal, as your life fulfils all that is required. Genitos, Julia would be very proud of you."

Standing up, Genitos shed happy tears and embraced his father. "Thank you for your help, Father. By week's end, I will be ready to speak to the assembly."

Genitos spent countless silent hours contemplating his future amongst the garden sculptures or walking the garden paths with his father, discussing his thoughts. Sitting together with his mother, he reminisced about all his adventures—and misadventures—of the past years. Her calmness quieted him as he prepared for the challenge ahead.

The day for his speech arrived quickly. The assembly hall vibrated with anticipation of the election of one of four qualified men.

Pedaeus, as the assembly leader, called each one in turn to the podium. Exactly as the bell sounded, signifying that the sun was at its highest, he announced the fourth and last speaker, Genitos.

Genitos straightened his shoulders, walked confidently up to the podium, and paused to acknowledge his audience and collect his thoughts.

Taking a deep breath, he began. "Assembly leader Pedaeus, and members of Salonica's city-state assembly, I humbly stand before you and thank you for allowing me to speak to this esteemed group in order to ask you to appoint me to be the honoured ambassador of our great city-state in Rome. My background enhances my ability to serve you in this honoured position like no one else.

"I was born in Salonica to Pedaeus and Anthela. As a well-educated young man with high ideals, and as an army officer, I fought for the freedom of this city. During one ferocious battle, I was captured and the Romans placed me in chains, after which they transported me to Rome and sold me as a slave.

"Romulus, the senior senator of Rome, bought me and had me race his chariots at Circus Maximus. I worked hard both mentally and physically to become the most winning, celebrated hero there. I was also forced to attend every political celebration, because the elite all wanted to brag that they had met me, talked to me, or shaken my hand. Thus I met most politicians and the wealthy men and women of Roman society. Over the years I learned humility, patience, and perseverance, tempered with the knowledge of dealing with Roman society.

"As time went on, I was accused of a crime of which I was innocent, and my owner banished me to the farthest part of the Roman Empire where I was purchased by Emontial, a wealthy Jewish businessman. At first I was his chariot driver, but later, after he became a follower of Jesus, he appointed me manager of all his factories, the mentor of his adoptive son Eronte, and the driver of Sheik Ostis al-Hussein's Arabian horses. Eventually he granted me freedom from slavery.

"I have extensive knowledge, not only of Greek and Roman, but also Jewish customs. My vast experiences in dealing with political ways of all three cultures will benefit Salonica. Be assured that I can handle any situations that come from this position. Therefore, in conclusion, I humbly offer my services to you, and ask that you appoint me as your ambassador to Rome."

Pedaeus, with a small, proud smile, dismissed the four applicants. "Thank you all for your presentations. You four gentlemen may leave the assembly room. We will not be asking you any further questions. We'll be in contact with a yea or a nay later this day. Thank you all for your presence."

The other three speakers had also spoken with clarity, but the assembly, by a huge majority, voted for Genitos. When he was called back to the assembly hall late that afternoon, Genitos was appointed in a ceremony to the honoured position of Salonica's ambassador to Rome.

Over a glass of rich, sweet Greek wine, the assembly members toasted Genitos' political appointment. "To Genitos! Our new ambassador to Rome! Congratulations, young man! Here, here!"

After the celebration, Genitos left the assembly hall with his father's arm round his shoulder. He was bouncing, a spring in his steps.

"Son, let us rush to tell your mother the results," Pedaeus said. "She will be so very pleased."

When they had arrived home, Genitos ran up the steps. "Mother, I wish you had been there! The excitement, cheers, and clapping resounded off the walls and ceiling. Everyone thumped my back and pumped my hands with great sincerity. I know I'll be an excellent ambassador."

She smiled in the direction of her husband. "Yes, son, I know you will be."

During the jubilant evening discussion, father, mother, and son decided they would prepare to travel to Rome together.

"Father, Mother, I am a very fortunate man," Genitos said. "The head magistrate of Rome has provided me with a war galley. We must travel as soon as possible, as I wish you to meet my Julia. Can you be ready five days hence?"

"Five days!" his mother exclaimed. "Did you say five days? Oh, so much to plan! But don't worry, son, I'll have your father ready."

Genitos called for his herald and dictated a message for the captain of the galley: "Captain, prepare galley for travel to Rome. My father and mother will have return passage with me. We intend to depart the port of Salonica on the morning of the fifth day hence." After the herald repeated the message, Genitos dismissed him. "Deliver my message to the captain of the galley anchored next to the port authority."

The morning of the fifth day dawned cloudless, with a steady breeze from the north. Feeling the wind in his hair, Pedaeus remarked, "Hurry now, Anthela, for this will be a fair sailing day."

"I'm on my way," she replied. "Only one more bag to finish. Let me see. Oh, so much to remember! Don't rush me!"

The captain and three sailors arrived to haul the baggage. After greetings all around, the travellers headed with great anticipation towards the harbour. Once safely aboard, they stood on deck while the captain shouted his orders: "Row out of the harbour, set the main sail into the wind, and head for Rome."

Genitos paced the deck like a caged tiger. His heart pounded as thoughts of Julia filled his mind. *I wish this boat would go faster! I can't wait to see Julia to tell her that I've solved our problem! We can be together! We* will *be together!*

Four days later, the galley was tethered to a dock in the harbour at Rome.

"Father, Mother, I'm leaving right now to see Julia," Genitos said with anticipation in his voice. "I cannot wait any longer to tell her the news! The captain will bring you to her home."

Jumping off the galley, he barely missed slipping into the water in his haste.

He arrived at her stately home and ran up the steps, bolting through the front door into her sitting room, where he met an astonished Julia. Before she could react, Genitos wrapped his arms tightly around her.

"Darling Julia, you are being hugged and kissed by the ambassador of the great city-state of Salonica," he seductively whispered in her ear. "I am now your equal, free to make love to you."

"Ambassador! What amazing news! The Roman elite will accept us now. We can be together!" Her voice changed from high excitement to quiet tenderness. "Genitos, I love you and will be yours forever."

Both knew what they desired to do, something they had refrained from before, to show their love for each other. Genitos picked her up gently and carried her to a room where they could enjoy each other in private. Time seemed not to exist as they made love.

Julia's house servant, knowing what was going on, rapped discretely at the door and announced when Genitos' parents had arrived. Getting dressed and grooming quickly, they both went out onto the porch with almost embarrassed smiles on their faces.

Genitos introduced his parents to Julia, and he could sense them chuckling to themselves as they remembered similar youthful times. Julia welcomed them by hugging his mother and kissing his father lightly on both cheeks.

They sat together on the porch, enjoying a time of companionship. A luncheon of fruit and fish was served during which his parents toasted their son and Julia with glasses of wine. They also discussed the newly empowered young lovers' wedding. The parents were entirely thrilled with Julia.

As the day drew to a close, Pedaeus remarked, "Julia, you are a very beautiful and kind lady. My son has made a wise choice. It is obvious you are both deeply in love. We will be very happy to have you in our family."

FORTY-ONE

Twenty-Eight Days

After the eventful happenings on race day, Convictus once again concentrated on his evil plans. The third and fourth court days passed painfully for him, with his suspense increasing. Convictus felt assured he would be the victor and that Emontial would become his slave. On the fifth and final morning, decision day, the sky darkened with black as night clouds as Convictus arrived at the courthouse. Convictus sat on a stone bench, smiling with gratification, and waited impatiently for the judgment.

Two tall legionnaires in red dress uniforms appeared and led Convictus through the courtroom to the bench where all seven magistrates were seated.

The head magistrate spoke in an authoritative voice. "We seven magistrates have made a final decree in your case against Emontial. Our unanimous decision is that you are obligated for the next twenty-eight days to follow in detail the ruling of this court, and then appear before Tribune Narcellus at the slavery court. The following is this court's ruling:

"One, Eronte was free before he became your personal slave. Therefore, Eronte will be your personal slave every day from sunup until sundown. From sundown until sunup, Eronte will spend his time at Emontial's home, free to do as he wishes.

"Two, you, Convictus, will never become inebriated.

"Three, you, Convictus, will treat everyone as you would like to be treated.

"Four, here is an official yellow scroll which you will deliver to Narcellus at dawn in the morning twenty-eight days from today. You must not open or tamper with the scroll in any way. If any sign—I repeat, any sign—of opening or tampering with this scroll is detected, your case will close instantly. Eronte, Paulus, and Marlan will then be immediately freed."

"B–but what about Emontial?" Convictus stammered.

The head magistrate pounded his gavel on the bench. "You have heard the final judgment of this court. This case is mandated."

The seven magistrates all stood and left the courtroom, one behind the other in a single row with the head magistrate leading.

Convictus, seething with anger, knew he was obligated to comply and follow the instructions of the court. He took the yellow scroll in hand and shook his head in disbelief.

When Convictus and Eronte returned home to Jerusalem, Convictus reluctantly followed the ruling exactly. In the evenings, he downed one or two glasses of wine rather than drink the whole flask as per usual.

His false outward smile and kind treatment of his slaves surprised all who knew of his cruel ways. He allotted them extra time in the evenings to enjoy substantial meals, and gave them time off from their various duties. Convictus was even heard to praise a slave. Unheard of! Passersby on the street were greeted with cordial conversation.

No one could believe the change. Everyone thought Convictus had become a better person, but little did they know his inner hatred against Emontial. Convictus was more determined than ever to decimate his adversary.

Time trudged by at a snail's pace. Exactly at dawn on the twenty-eighth day, Convictus went to the slavery court and carefully withdrew the official yellow scroll from within his robe. He presented it to Tribune Narcellus, who turned the scroll over, examining it minutely, and found it had not been tampered with.

Unrolling the scroll, Narcellus read it carefully, then scrutinized Convictus' cold eyes. "Convictus, I'm going to ask you one simple question to which your only answer will be yes or no. You must not answer the question until I instruct you to answer. If you respond before I direct you, this case will be closed, and as a result Eronte, Paulus, and Marlan will be freed. Do you understand everything I have told you?"

"I have understood every word, but I do have one request."

"What is it? My instructions on the scroll state emphatically that this question must be read to you at the sound of the bell when the sun is at its highest. When I signal you to answer, you must answer immediately."

Convictus continued with false humility. "May you read me the question on the platform at the stadium? I plan to hold a party to celebrate, and I intend to provide free food and drink for all guests who attend. I have built a solid wooden platform twenty paces above the racetrack. It stretches from the outer wall onto the spina, one hundred paces in length."

"You have the remainder of the morning to make preparations," Narcellus said, "but I can see no reason why I couldn't ask you the question on the platform."

"Thank you, Tribune. I will be there precisely at the appointed time. Please, see that Emontial is there. I will bring Eronte, Paulus, and Marlan."

* * *

That very morning, knowing he might not be in Eronte's company again, Emontial unlocked the small, secluded chest hidden beneath his desk. He'd had it specially built to protect all his prized possessions. Emontial withdrew the relic he was most honoured to preserve: Jesus Christ's sandals in the satchel with the wide leather shoulder strap.

He woke Eronte gently as dawn arrived. "Eronte, here are Christ's sandals. I thank you for giving me the honour of lovingly preserving them and making me aware of how happy I am to be alive. Because of them, I learned to believe in the teachings of Jesus and become a Christian. I now know how to treat my neighbour as myself."

"Emontial, I'll never forget you," Eronte said. "I thank you from the bottom of my heart for all your caring love. I hope I will see you again!"

As they shared breakfast together, their time was bittersweet and filled with warm memories that would linger once they parted. Then Eronte, without a backward glance, left carrying over his shoulder the leather bag with the sandals.

Convictus rushed to his office from the courthouse to make sure all preparations were in order and that his slaves had invited everyone to view his victory. He then went home hastily to triumphantly collect Eronte,

Paulus, and Marlan, who accompanied him solemnly to the platform at the stadium, wondering what fate their cruel owner had in store for them.

Tribune Narcellus and Emontial were waiting for Convictus. With yellow scroll in hand, Narcellus prepared to ask the one question that would impact the lives of many people. Convictus stared at the gathered crowd, noticing that Eronte was wearing a satchel over his shoulder. He intensely disliked when the young man dressed like a free man.

Exactly as the bell sounded, Narcellus unrolled the yellow scroll. "Convictus, remember that you must answer the question immediately when I signal, but only when I signal and not before."

With only the hint of a snarl in his voice, Convictus responded with false sweetness. "Before you signal me to answer, would you please allow me to have my slave Eronte dressed properly as a slave?"

Narcellus nodded, a decided edginess in his voice. "Do it quickly!"

Convictus swung his hand to slap Eronte for wearing the satchel, but he lost his balance and started to fall from the platform. Eronte, with strength and agility, reacted quickly and caught Convictus' ankle with his left hand, holding him awkwardly as he dangled in the air.

"Save me!" Convictus cried out. "Don't let me go! I don't want to fall! Or be killed! Or maimed! Eronte, use your strength! Pull me back to the podium! Please, save my life! Please! Please, don't let me fall! I beg you! Save me! I am sorry for how I have treated you and your family and Emontial. I promise that I will free all of you and treat everyone with kindness. Believe me, I beg you, please pull me up! Save me! I will do whatever you wish!"

Eronte swung Convictus back and forth in the open air. "Why should I allow you to live? If I let you fall, we will all be free of your cruel treatment."

Convictus screamed, yelled, and begged. "I'll give up everything I own if you save me."

"How do I know you'll do as you say? You didn't change at Circus Maximus when your life was in danger."

"I will! I will! I will! Save me!"

Eronte yanked Convictus up to a point where he could grab the man's other ankle. With his great strength, Ertone raised him up and placed him upright on the platform. But he kept Convictus' arm in his tight grasp.

"It's ironic, Convictus, that your harsh treatment of me as your slave—making me run behind your carruca, making me lift and carry all the heavy loads—gave me the strength to save you. The teaching of Jesus gave me the opportunity to forgive you and treat you as I would want to be treated."

FORTY-TWO

Revelation Redemption

"You slapped me just because I'm wearing this satchel," Eronte continued. "I'll tell you why I wear it, and why I saved you just now."

Eronte took the wide leather strap carefully off his shoulder and handed it over to Convictus, who placed his hand on the bag and roughly opened the flap. He put his other hand into the satchel and pulled out Jesus Christ's sandals.

"What are these?" Convictus asked, examining them carefully. "They look ordinary to me. They're not new. What's significant about these worthless sandals?"

"Well, Convictus, years ago I watched the agony of a teacher and healer named Jesus as He was crucified, and the forgiveness He showed for Treatorus the legionnaire who nailed Him to the cross. Jesus said, 'Forgive them, Father, for they know not what they do.' Treatorus, feeling pangs of guilt, desired to do some good. Seeing me, a poor, homeless boy, he decided to give me the crucified man's sandals. He told me to sell them to get money to buy food. These sandals remind me what Jesus taught: to forgive and treat others as I would like to be treated."

"Yes, Convictus," Emontial added. "That same day, I was beaten almost to death by four of my tenants. Even in my pain, I was given the opportunity to do right or wrong, to follow the teachings of Jesus or not. These sandals represent the love that is Jesus. I treasure them because I think they somehow provide opportunities for a person to do the right thing—or not—in following the teachings of the man who owned them."

"The change in Emontial occurred as I placed Jesus' sandals on him when he was beaten and lying on the ground," Eronte interjected. "Then he learned the Christian way of life. Right now you tried to slap me, and you slipped, falling from the platform. I had the choice of saving you or letting you drop. These sandals reminded me what Jesus taught, so I grabbed your other ankle and saved you."

Gently placing the treasured sandals back into the satchel, Convictus closed the flap and placed the wide leather strap over Eronte's shoulder.

"This satchel belongs to you, Eronte," Convictus said. He dropped to his knees in front of Eronte and, with a bowed head, thanked him for saving his life. He apologized loudly, in front of all the gathered people, to Emontial, Paulus, Marlan, and Eronte for his cruel behaviour.

He then turned his attention back to Tribune Narcellus with a complete change of personality. "I am ready! Please, signal me to answer that important question."

Narcellus began reading the scroll. "Roman law states that every child born of a female slave is considered to be a slave owned by the female slave's owner." He motioned to Emontial, but directed his words to Convictus. "This celebrated person, Emontial, broke the law. You, Convictus, owned the female slave Marlan, who had a son called Eronte. Emontial unknowingly at first, then later knowingly, committed a crime against the Empire. Is that correct?"

Both Emontial and Convictus nodded in agreement.

"Therefore, Convictus, the high court's decision will depend only on how you answer the following question, yes or no. Do you want this court to rule in your favour to punish Emontial to the fullest extent of the law?"

Convictus stared directly at Narcellus. He raised his arms and shouted, "No! No!"

"Convictus, your answer satisfies the judgment of this court." Narcellus then turned to the expectant crowd to pronounce his final ruling. "Emontial, you are in no danger of being enslaved. The charge against you is null and void. Paulus, Marlan, and Eronte are free to live their lives in the happiness you, Emontial, have provided."

Convictus smiled pleasantly and approached Emontial with humility. Speaking in a voice loud enough for all to hear, he apologized for his cruel behaviour. "Emontial, my friend, please forgive me."

The two men embraced.

"God bless you, Convictus. Praise be to Jesus, for the power of the miracle he provided through His sandals." Emontial continued praising loudly for all to hear. "The two most important commandments of Jesus' teaching, if followed, will bring joy to everyone. The first commandment being, 'Love God with all your heart, all your soul, and all your mind.' And the second commandment is 'Love your neighbour as yourself,' because if you love God, you will desire to treat your neighbour as you would like to be treated.'"

The crowd cheered and clapped in appreciation.

"Well said," Eronte agreed.

Emontial reached out for Eronte's left hand and Convictus grabbed the right. The three walked joyfully down the steps of the raised platform and marched right to the centre of Jerusalem, gently parting the cheering crowd as they passed.

FORTY-THREE

An Ambassador Returns

Learning that Genitos had returned to Rome as the ambassador of Salonica, Sheik Ostis al-Hussein went directly to Julia's home. He met Genitos on the porch, grabbed him, and hugged him.

"Wonderful to see you looking so happy, and so strong," al-Hussein said. "Tell me the whole story of what happened."

"I gained equality with the Roman elite by being appointed the Salonican ambassador. Now Julia and I can be together."

"Do you have a place to stay?"

"Yes, I have my embassy, or I can stay here at Julia's home. But I prefer to remain at the embassy until we're married."

"I have a home on the outskirts of Rome that I bought with the money we made from racing," al-Hussein told him. "You're welcome to stay there and treat it as your own. Consider this my wedding present to you both. Actually, Genitos, you helped to pay for this very palatial home by winning all those races."

"Thank you. I'll accept your hospitality."

"All I ask in return is that you race my pet Arabians when you have time."

"I would love to." Genitos then turned and introduced him to his parents. "Father, Mother, please meet my friend, Sheik Ostis al-Hussein, the sheik of Ziz. He's the owner of the horses I told you about. Sheik Ostis, these are my parents, Pedaeus and Anthela."

"It's a pleasure to meet you both!"

Al-Hussein encircled Genitos' shoulders with his arms. "Your son, I love like a son. He has made me proud of my life in Rome. He is the most celebrated charioteer ever to race at Circus Maximus."

Anthela gave him a wide smile. "We think he is very special too."

Julia tiptoed up behind Genitos, hugged him, and flashed a smile of her own. "Yes, very special! Hi, Ostis. So nice to see you again! I'm so happy that my love is back. We plan to marry, but we'll wait until Genitos is fully competent in his new appointment."

"You look beautiful with your eyes shining so brightly," al-Hussein said. "There is so much happiness here. I must return now to prepare my home for you. Remember, Genitos, it is yours for as long as you like. I will be honoured for you to live there."

Genitos clasped him on the shoulders with both hands. "Thank you, my friend, for your kindness."

FORTY-FOUR

Wedding Plans

On the thirty-first day of Quintilis, Legalus visited Julia and Genitos at high sun. Sitting together under the garden portico and enjoying a glass of wine, he spoke to them in a solemn tone.

"Genitos and Julia, my official visit today will see that you both fulfill the three main aspects of your marriage—the legal, the social, and the religious. You have fulfilled the legal with the iron ring being given by Genitos to you, Julia, and in return you stated your verbal consent. Also, you both presented each other with gifts and sums of money. The social aspect will be fulfilled at the festive party the day following Calends Sextilis, when the actual ceremony will take place."

Although the two had their eyes riveted on the magistrate, both appeared somewhat dreamy, with hands clasped and fingers entwined. The magistrate wasn't sure if the young couple was paying attention.

"Listen carefully to my instructions," he said. "The religious feature is very important and is held in the middle of the afternoon. Genitos, you will head to your home to receive your bride. Julia, you will light a torch in your hearth and carry it with you to Genitos' home. Outside the door of Genitos' home, you will be offered another torch, and also water, symbolizing *aquae et ignis communicato*. At this point, Julia, you will be carried over the threshold by your attendants, not by Genitos. The words 'Ubi tu Gaius, ibi ego Gaia' will be said by both of you. You will stay together that night in Genitos' house. The actual consummation of your marriage will take place in the bedroom in the dark after you are alone. Do you have any questions?"

Both were silent as they nodded, still staring at each other with love in their eyes.

Genitos broke the silence first. "Thank you for telling us the exact features of the wedding, and the ceremonies. We will follow exactly what you have taught us."

"Until tomorrow!" the magistrate said. "It thrills my heart that you two are so happy, knowing all too well what could have been."

FORTY-FIVE

The News Spreads

To his happy surprise, al-Hussein encountered Emontial's herald in the courtyard upon arriving at his palatial home to prepare for Genitos.

"Speak!"

The herald delivered Emontial's message: "Ostis, have excellent news for you. Convictus has set all of us—Marlan, Paulus, Eronte, and myself—completely free from slavery. We are travelling to Rome shortly. When I see you, will explain in detail what transpired to bring about this happy outcome. The circumstances were unbelievable. Best wishes, Emontial."

"Return with my message to Emontial," al-Hussein said, and then began to dictate: "Emontial! Wonderful news! Can't wait to hear details! Have pleasant news for you. Genitos is back in Rome as ambassador of Salonica and is now of the finest elite class. Intends to marry Julia. You are all invited. Expect Genitos' wedding invitation to arrive soon. Come with haste after receiving invitation. Genitos' and Julia's wedding will be quite a celebration. All Roman elite, especially the high ups, are almost begging for an invitation. Will fill you in further upon your arrival. Hope to see you as soon as possible. And please, see that Convictus is invited also. As ever, Ostis."

Upon receiving the sheik's message, Emontial rushed to Convictus' office.

"Convictus, we are to be invited to a wedding," Emontial said. "We are going to gather up Paulus, Marlan, and Eronte and sail to Rome as soon as we know the specific plans."

"Slow down, my friend. Take a breath. You are so excited."

"Yes, yes, I am! I just received word from Sheik Ostis al-Hussein. Genitos is now the ambassador to Rome from Salonica, and we have to hurry to be in time to attend Genitos' and Julia's wedding."

"Well, that is happy news."

"Yes, and we all must go, especially you, to show everyone that we all follow Christ's teaching to forgive people for what they have done wrong, and treat our neighbours as we would like to be treated. And I want you to attend the chariot races at Circus Maximum with Genitos racing the white Arabians. We will have fun together, all of us!"

"Sounds like a good opportunity to show our love for each other," Convictus agreed. "Are you sure I am invited? I will go on only one condition: that I pay for everything to thank you all for making my life content as never before."

"Well! That's a deal! Thank you! It's certainly not necessary, but yes, I will accept your offer. When can you be ready to travel? We can't waste any time."

"I can be ready by daybreak fourteen days hence."

Emontial waved over his shoulder as he departed. "Goodbye, Convictus, I will let you know the further plans. See you soon."

Thinking to himself how things had changed, Emontial hurried home. Without stopping for a breath, he called out, "Paulus, Marlan, Eronte, begin to prepare. We are going to Rome to participate in Genitos' and Julia's wedding."

All three entered the room and stood still as statues, digesting the news. Then pandemonium erupted.

"I thought the elite wouldn't speak to them and would ruin their lives," Eronte said.

"Genitos now has a high position in the Greek government. I'll explain later. Hurry, make preparations!"

Marlan and Paulus looked at Emontial with huge smiles.

"We're thrilled beyond belief," Marlan said exuberantly. "What can we do to help you and Eronte get ready to travel to Rome?"

"Eronte and I? No, no, you misunderstand, Marlan. You and Paulus are also invited, and Convictus, to attend the wedding. It will be the event of the season and you'll meet many of my close friends and acquaintances there."

Eronte couldn't contain himself. A smile beamed from his every pore. "Emontial, I'm leaving for Rome immediately. I must arrive there with haste."

After a warm-hearted goodbye with Emontial and his parents, Eronte went to his room. He eagerly packed, then made arrangements to travel to Asquelon the next morning to board the galley that would ferry him to Rome and Genitos.

Eronte was already en route when another herald appeared at Emontial's door before the evening meal was laid out. This one bore the official wedding invitation from Genitos.

"Genitos and Julia wish you, Emontial and Eronte, to attend their wedding and all festivities," the herald announced stiffly. "Please include Paulus, Marlan, and especially Convictus in this invitation. The wedding date is Calends Sextilis. Please arrive here early, sometime around Quintilis Ides."

Emontial thanked him. "Herald, return to Rome with the following message to Genitos: Thank you. Everyone pleased to accept your invitation. Will arrive on or before Quintilis Ides. Bursting with happiness for you and Julia. Sincere congratulations. Emontial."

The next morning, before the sun reached the treetops, Emontial again rushed to Convictus' office.

"Emontial, calm yourself. What brings you here in such a panic? You're out of breath, your eyes are popping out of your head, and you're speaking too fast for me. What has happened?"

"Convictus, send for Paulus and Marlan, so they may join us in arranging travel plans," Emontial said. "Quickly, pour us glasses of your best wine."

"Quit bouncing, Emontial," Convictus said. "Here, hold these wine glasses and I'll pour. What is this celebration about?"

Emontial continued in a rush. "Quiet! I have received official word from Genitos and I'm to invite you to his wedding in Rome on Calends Sextilis. I plan to have us all there, if you can go, by or before Ides Quintilis."

"Am I really invited, even after all the pain I caused?"

"Yes, Convictus. Genitos and Julia specifically invited you. Be happy that you have changed from being one of the cruellest men in Jerusalem to one of the finest, through following the teachings of Christ. I often wonder what would have become of us all if Eronte hadn't helped me with the sandals of Christ that day so many years ago."

"All right then, I will go. But only, as I said before, if you allow me to sponsor the entire trip."

With thanks and hands clasped, the four discussed their travel plans.

FORTY-SIX:

The Guests Arrive

Quivering with excitement at the day ahead, Eronte rose before sun's blush and set off. The private galley, which he had dispatched his herald to hire, was ready to go with its sails unfurled when he arrived at the dock.

"My destination is Rome," Eronte instructed the captain. "Travel swiftly. I'm impatient to see and talk to my best friend, Genitos, and find out personally what has been happening in his world! And when his wedding will take place! And everything! I'm overjoyed!"

"It's now the five Ides of Martius," the captain said. "The weather seems to be good and the wind is favourable. With good passage, we should be on land four days hence."

"Just do your best, and I will reward you and your men for their hard work."

"Yes, I will do my best, but I have only the wind and excellent sailors. I freed my galley slaves years ago."

"Captain, the faster you get this galley to Rome, the more denarii I will pay you. I am beside myself! I'm so excited! My friend is free from slavery, is now an ambassador, and plans to marry a woman he couldn't before because he was her slave."

"I can understand your urgency. Go, sit on the starboard deck. Have a tall glass of my fine wine. I'll join you shortly. I'd like to hear more, but we'll get underway now. My men and I will sail this galley as smoothly, steadily, and speedily as it can travel."

The galley docked at Rome exactly four days later. Eronte paid the captain and his men three times the fare.

After arranging for delivery of his baggage, he rushed to Julia's home. His feet barely touched ground as he hurried up the porch and knocked on the door.

"Genitos, I couldn't wait to see you after hearing all the good news."

Both men spoke excitedly. "Eronte, what a thrilling and wonderful surprise! How did you know to come?"

"Sheik Ostis sent his herald to Emontial with your news."

"And my own herald is en route and should be in Jerusalem by now! Please meet my love, Julia."

Julia kissed Eronte lightly on both cheeks and welcomed him to her home. Genitos shook his hands and hugged him so hard he could barely breathe.

Wiping happy tears from their eyes, the trio ambled into the garden and strolled leisurely up and down. Time seemed to stand still as they told each other of their lives.

"Genitos and I were just discussing plans for our wedding feast," Julia said. "It will be here in the garden of my home, and I'm planning all sorts of wonderful delicacies to eat."

"When is the wedding to take place?" Eronte asked. "Emontial, Paulus, Marlan, and even Convictus want to celebrate with you."

Giddy with the joy of the moment, Julia interjected before Genitos could open his mouth. "The date is set for Calends Sextilis." She lifted her hand, danced, and waved her hand in front of Eronte's eyes. "See! This iron ring signifies our commitment to marry. I love it! We're going to have the wedding where Genitos lives. For our wedding present, Ostis generously gave Genitos his palatial home on the outskirts of Rome. We're already exchanging gifts, money, and personal items, as is the Roman custom, before our marriage."

Genitos looked at his darling with love in his eyes. He placed two fingers in a hush gesture over his mouth, thus changing the tone of the conversation.

"I do hope Convictus accepts my invitation," Genitos said solemnly. "He is beneficial for the soul because he will demonstrate to Ostis, Legalus, and all who have met his wrath that he really has changed."

"And to think this whole process began when I received Jesus' sandals from Treatorus," Eronte said as they continued their walk through the garden. "As a result, not only did Emontial change, but Convictus also now treats others as he would like to be treated."

* * *

With the exception of the laughter and chatter of the four passengers on board Convictus' galley, the voyage across the Mediterranean was calm, quiet, and rather uneventful. Convictus, Emontial, Marlan, and Paulus arrived in Rome and docked on four Ides Quintilis. Convictus, true to his word, paid for everything: he hired a carruca and directed the driver to transport them to Julia's house.

They reached the house as quickly as possible, then excitedly disembarked and rushed into the garden.

"Genitos, Eronte, Julia? Where are you?" Emontial called. "We're here!"

Around the corner of the courtyard, with huge smiles on their faces, Genitos and Julia rushed toward them. Introductions, greetings, hugs, and kisses ensued. Hands in hands and arms wrapped around shoulders, they walked hurriedly to the porch where everyone sat down. Glasses of wine seemed to appear out of nowhere and the exuberant conversation continued for hours.

Finally, Genitos stood up. "I know you're tired. We'll continue this conversation in the morning. Right now, I'll have the carruca driver transport you all to my home where my servants have a meal ready and sleeping quarters prepared for you to have a restful night. I'll follow along presently. You will see Eronte tomorrow. Today, he's off arranging plans with the head magistrate for the wedding festivities. He'll be very excited to hear you arrived safely."

Thanking Julia for her hospitality, they shook hands in appreciation and travelled to Genitos' home to relax in comfort for the night.

The next morning dawned with warm sun bathing the gardens as they breakfasted on the porch with Eronte, who had bounded in before first light. The day to follow was filled with adventures as Convictus toured them through Rome, winding up at Circus Maximus where Genitos once again raced al-Hussein's Arabian stallions, defeating Marvellus. The travellers, entertained by Convictus, enjoyed every day in Rome.

FORTY-SEVEN

Wedding Day Ceremony and Festivities

Calends Sextilis dawned a beautiful day. With the sun at its highest, Genitos walked over to see Julia. She looked dazzling, standing in the doorway. Genitos gently hugged her and kissed her firmly on the lips.

"I will love you forever," he said. "You are the most beautiful girl in the world."

And then he left her to go ahead, as was the custom.

Julia, with her attendant's assistance, lit a torch in her fireplace's hearth and carried it to Genitos' home. Moving slowly but with purposeful steps, Julia held the lighted torch high. When she arrived, she met Genitos who received her torch and gave her a different lit torch with a jar of water, symbolizing *aquae et ignis communicato*.

Her attendants then carried her across the threshold and put her down inside.

"Ubi tu Gaius, ibi ego Gaia," the couple spoke in unison. As they hugged, all the attendants left. Later that night, they consummated their being together for eternity.

They arose the next morning, kissed each other affectionately, and with loving words prepared for the feast part of their marriage celebration.

Genitos put his arm around his wife. "Julia, I will always be your protector. I will never leave you. I'm so grateful for your love."

"As I am for your love, Genitos."

Hand in hand, and staring dreamily into each other's eyes, they walked to Julia's home for the grand party which by custom was to be held at the bride's home, with the groom looking after all the expenses.

The elite of Rome had all clambered for an invitation to this very elaborate party. It was ironic; these same persons who once would have shunned Genitos and Julia now begged for an invitation to the most esteemed social gathering of the year.

Julia couldn't count the guests, for many appeared to wish them well, even without an invitation. She estimated that at least a thousand visitors crowded the main rooms, squeezing into every corner of the garden and courtyard. Everyone wanted to congratulate the couple. Even the Emperor Caligula, to everyone's surprise, arrived as the sumptuous meal was about to be served.

There was an audible intake of breath from the guests as Caligula entered the large room. His legionnaires prepared and raised a plushly padded chair for the Emperor to sit above all the other guests.

Genitos and Julia waited until after Caligula signalled his legionnaires to have them approach. The couple didn't know what to expect, as Caligula was known for violent and irrational outbursts. Walking slowly up to the Emperor, they both bowed.

"Welcome, Emperor Caligula," Genitos said. "We are honoured to see you here at our wedding feast. We hope that you enjoy our hospitality, the meal, and the party."

At that moment, Eronte walked close to the Emperor carrying his satchel containing Christ's sandals. A softer, kinder demeanour came over the ruler.

Could it be the influence of Christ emanating from His sandals? Eronte wondered.

Caligula turned his attention to Julia. "Julia, you are absolutely beautiful."

Still clutching Genitos' hand while bowing low, Julia answered, "I thank you for your kind comment."

"Genitos, listen to me carefully," the Emperor said, "for I am feeling strangely generous and happy at the moment. I wasn't going to give you any advice, but now I will. Being an ambassador, especially from a Greek city-state, will be a difficult task due to the fact that you personally fought against Rome. Several senators remember that. They also know that you were Julia's slave, and some are jealous of your fame as a charioteer. As the supreme ruler, I appreciate your courage and honesty. If you ever need advice, bring this yellow stone to my palace and you will be ushered into my presence immediately. Whatever the difficulty, I will solve it for you as only I can as Emperor."

Bowing low in appreciation, Genitos acknowledged the Emperor's gift. "Thank you. You honour me not only with your presence here today, but with your kindness towards Julia and your trust in my ability. We are most grateful for your gift, Emperor Caligula. Please, enjoy our hospitality."

The guests looked at each other in disbelief. They, too, had heard but questioned why the Emperor had spoken these kindnesses. All present gave a collective sigh of relief as the party continued.

The gustus, or appetizers, were served on ornately designed platters which filled the tables. They consisted of assorted meats and nuts, wild fruit, and various figs, olives, grapes, dates, and breads. Seafood had been cooked with leeks in white wine. Melons drizzled with honey and pear soufflé added a touch of sweetness to the beginning of the meal.

The main course consisted of pork, goat, chicken, grouse, and rabbit, and the most luxurious and expensive meat, beef. Even dormouse, the greatest delicacy, was on the menu. The cherished foul, peacock, was served on plates. Accompanying these meats were the vegetables—artichokes, beans, asparagus, beets, onions, fennel, and garlic.

Dessert consisted of fruit and nuts. Grapes, apples, pears, plums, hazelnuts, almonds, walnuts, and pistachios were arranged and stacked like small mountains on carved wooden platters in the centre of the tables. The guests consumed fine wine made from grapes, berries, and other fruits.

Musicians played the flute and panpipes during the meal. Guests sang, danced, and read poetry. Jugglers, musicians, and magicians entertained. The festivities lasted for many hours.

This wedding celebration was one of the largest in Rome's history.

* * *

As the years passed, Genitos continued to race for Sheik Ostis al-Hussein and was very successful and respected as the youngest foreign ambassador to Rome. He and Julia raised three beautiful children and lived long, happy lives.

Marlan, Paulus, and Convictus continued to purchase and sell expensive wares in their shops, but they also distributed robes and other basic goods to people in need. Convictus became known as a benefactor to many in Jerusalem and beyond.

And as for Emontial, and Eronte? The younger managed the two chariot factories and oversaw business ventures for the elder statesman, who continued to share the story of how Jesus' wonderful sandals, in the hands of a caring young boy, had changed his life forever, and the joy brought by learning about the Messiah who had worn those sandals. They continued to keep safe the sandals of Christ, treasuring them as a symbol of Jesus' love.

Near the end of his life, Eronte placed Christ's sandals in the care of Jesus' disciple Paul, honouring an earlier request by Emontial.

Epilogue

"What an incredible story!" Lynne exclaimed. "These sandals we're holding, Dad, belonged to Christ Himself! Through the miraculous power of Jesus, these sandals seemed to provide people opportunities to make the right decisions to help others in distress at the crux of their need."

Henry smiled at his daughter. "Yes, Lynne. Imagine what the world would be like if everyone followed Christ's teachings. The battle between good and evil still continues. My question is this: why did Jesus' sandals fall beside me at the ruins of the old abbey? What do we do with them now?"

"Dad, could it be that God wants you to use Christ's power through His miraculous sandals to somehow share His love with others to heal the world of its present woes?"

Where did the sandals journey with Paul? How did the sandals pass from Eronte's safekeeping to parts unknown until ending up in St. Stephen's church? Those parts of the story remain to be told.

This is not the end of the story, but again the beginning.

About the Author

W. Paul Elgie, B.A., B.Ed., M. Ed., is a retired educator who has garnered a lifetime of experiences and ideas over his eighty years ranging from education, music, theatre, and community service. As a high school teacher, he taught primarily senior English and Drama, produced and directed musicals, and officiated as an adult and summer school principal. He was appointed by the Ontario Ministry of Education to act as an advisor for the Ontario drama curriculum.

He has composed music for piano and enjoys playing in churches. His signature hymn is "How Great Thou Art." He studied as a young man at the Pasadena Playhouse in California, and later put this knowledge to use as a broadcasting interviewer and theatrical critic.

Paul served as a steward and elder in his local church, and for twenty-five years he was lay pulpit supply for various churches. He also served as municipal councillor and was a member of the Ontario Library and Children's Aid boards.

Other interests include being a trained RCAF pilot, avid golfer, and traveler. As a child Paul's love of horses began with his pony "Dolly" and his family's riding show horses. This love of the majestic animal continued into adult life as Paul bred, raised, and raced Standbred horses. Paul and his wife Marilyn reside in the town of Goderich, Ontario.